Hiding from Hollywood

Ellie Darkins

CRIMSON ROMANCE
F+W Media, Inc.

This edition published by
Crimson Romance
an imprint of F+W Media, Inc.
10151 Carver Road, Suite 200
Blue Ash, Ohio 45242
www.crimsonromance.com

ISBN 10: 1-4405-7915-6
ISBN 13: 978-1-4405-7915-8
eISBN 10: 1-4405-7914-8
eISBN 13: 978-1-4405-7914-1

Acknowledgments

I couldn't have written this book without the help of a huge number of people. So, thanks go to all my friends and family for their support and patience, to Alexia Adams and Sarah Long for their insightful and infinitely helpful critiques and suggestions, and to Mike for all the tea. Finally, thanks to the whole team at Crimson for their enthusiasm and support for Abby and Ethan's story.

Chapter One

"Abby, get your butt out here!"

Abby licked her finger and scrubbed at the black smudges beneath her eyes, ignoring Candy calling her from the kitchen. She checked the results and sighed. No such luck. It wasn't mascara after all, just the color of her skin. Three double shifts in a row had clearly taken their toll. She applied another layer of concealer and groaned as she caught sight of her uniform.

The uniform of the Hollywood Diner was too everything: too short, too tight, too see-through. And worst of all, too clichéd. But Abby had to face facts. Her acting career was over, and like every other "resting" actor in Los Angeles, she was waiting tables.

Before she'd left England, the waitress uniform had haunted her dreams—though the one in her nightmares was nowhere near as bad as the real thing—but she never imagined that she might be grateful for it. She'd headed out here, full of excitement and expectation, buoyed up by her BAFTA nomination, her British Soap Awards gongs. She couldn't have foreseen that within weeks she'd have been forced out of her acting career and be hiding from the world.

There was no use feeling sorry for herself though; plenty of people were worse off. This job put food on the table, a roof over her head, and kept the bailiffs from the door. She should be grateful. She was grateful. She just had to remind herself of that fact from time to time.

"Abby!"

Last checks: tighten ponytail, pull down skirt to try and cover another half inch of thigh, paste on Hollywood Diner Smile. Ready for business. *Thank God her mum couldn't see her now,* she thought. Abby knew exactly what her mother would think of the sort of girl who wore this to work. It was typical of this city that she couldn't even serve burgers without giving her customers an eyeful of leg—though thankfully, at just five foot two, she didn't have too much leg to worry about.

"*Abby!*"

The kitchen was its usual combination of smoke, steam, heat, and cursing. On her first shift Abby had thought it was hell. She couldn't imagine what the devil could possibly have down there that was worse than this room. But two years on she could see that this wasn't chaos. Okay, so maybe that wasn't strictly true, but it was *organized* chaos. It had a tempo and a rhythm that was second nature to her now. And when she had really needed somewhere to hide out, this place had been here.

On the surface there was nothing remarkable about the diner. It looked like any other: peeling Formica tables, vinyl-covered benches, and a host of slightly greasy-looking regulars. In fact, the only thing that would mark it out from a hundred others was that it would be the shabbiest of the lot. The first time she'd seen it, it seemed like the perfect place to lie low for a while; all she'd wanted was somewhere quiet and out of the way. Somewhere no one with any profile in the movie business could stumble across her and ask questions. But after a few weeks, she'd realized that she wanted to stay. She couldn't go back to England—the tabloids and gossip blogs would be all over it, wondering why Britain's brightest young acting talent was back so soon, with no blockbuster to her name. And a new job or a new city meant more people knowing her face, her name—her legal one—the one she thought she'd said goodbye to the first time she'd seen Abby Richards on her Equity card.

So the likelihood of finding anywhere else that would make her feel as safe as this grungy old place was slim. And the thought of leaving, exposing herself to more people, more questions, kept her here. If any of the Hollywood elite—or, more likely, a D-list wannabe—stepped foot in here, they would be too concerned about the welfare of their Gucci loafers, and distracted by the suspicious-looking stains, to look closely at the waitresses.

"I'm here, what's the emergency?" Abby said, walking out into the restaurant.

"No emergency." Candy grinned from where she was standing behind the counter. "I was bored out here on my own, that's all. It's *quiet* today."

Abby rolled her eyes at her friend and walked over to the booth by the window. She started to clear the empty coffee cups, but was distracted by the sight of a sleek, black Aston Martin pulling up at the curb. Not the sort of car you saw every day—or ever—in this neighborhood. *Idiot,* she thought. It wouldn't last ten minutes parked out there before word spread among the neighborhood kids.

She continued watching the car, and her eyes widened as its driver climbed out. *It couldn't be* ... The resemblance was uncanny. He looked just like Ethan Walker—but there was no way a Hollywood producer would be in this part of town. That was the whole *point* of being in this part of town. She stared as he walked towards the diner and when he was ten feet away, she was certain it was him. He was all sharp cheekbones, chiseled jaw, and three-day stubble. Abby would recognize that face anywhere, every woman in the city probably would—it featured every week in the online gossip rags and trashy magazines, usually accompanied by some hot new actress. Abby held her breath as he came closer. Surely he wouldn't be coming in here.

Her cheeks warmed as he looked over and noticed her watching him from the window. Their eyes met, just for a second, and he smiled at her. Her feet were frozen. She had to move; she had to get out of here. And yet, one smile from him, and she couldn't put one foot in front of the other.

It's okay, she told herself as the bell rang and he stepped through the door. *In here, I'm a waitress. I'm just like every other waitress in the city. What are the chances he watches British soaps anyway? He doesn't know me. I'm safe.*

But he kept moving towards her, and reached out to shake her hand. Still frozen in place, she looked up at him.

"Abby Richards?"

With those two words, Abby wished she had lingered longer in the bathroom. She wished she had run out the back door. She wished that she had never come to this bloody country in the first place.

He knew who she was.

Her feet finally unstuck from the floor. She grabbed his outstretched hand and dragged him out the door, away from the window, and around the corner.

Abby tried to weigh up the damage. The door to the kitchen had swung shut just before Ethan walked in, so she didn't think Candy had seen him. She didn't think anyone else in the diner had had time to recognize him either—in jeans and a casual shirt his appearance didn't scream "millionaire Hollywood movie producer." But if he didn't leave, right now, her secret could be blown and the life she'd built for herself here would be over. How had he found her? *Why* had he found her? And more importantly, how was she going to get rid of him?

He was smiling at her. He had the nerve to stand there and smile at her when any second he was going to ruin her life—or what was left of it anyway.

Even now, though, angry and afraid, she couldn't help but notice his eyes, so dark they were almost black, twinkling at her from under ever-so-slightly-too-long hair. And the way the angles of his cheekbones and jaw fell with perfect balance and symmetry. It was the sort of anatomical perfection a girl just couldn't ignore, whatever the circumstances.

His jeans and shirt were understated, but they drew more attention to his body than an Armani tux. The white shirt highlighted his tan, just the right side of golden, and the open collar showed a hint of black hair disappearing below the neckline. The rolled sleeves exposed perfectly toned forearms and Abby's stomach clenched at the sight of the muscles there.

Ethan Walker leant against the wall in the stinking alley she'd dragged them to and gave her a questioning look.

"Miss Richards, my name is—"

"I know who you are." When she realized that she was still clenching his hand, she pulled away, though he tried to keep a hold of her. Determined to keep him at a distance, she crossed her arms in front of her body. Between her anger and attraction, she didn't quite trust herself not to do something with them that she might later regret.

It was painful to admit, even to herself (especially as he could be about to ruin the little of her life she'd managed to salvage), but he was hot. In two years, she hadn't given a man—any man—a second glance. She hadn't thought, after what had been done to her, that she would ever feel anything like it again. But something in her, something that had hidden, scared, was making tentative steps out towards the world, towards Ethan. Typical that the first man she'd felt even a spark of attraction for since her assault was not only the city's most notoriously confirmed bachelor, but also the man whose high profile could do her more harm than just about anyone else on the planet.

Keeping herself out of the limelight was the only way to keep safe. To stop the people who had hurt her once, who held the evidence of that hurt over her like a threat, from publishing those photos and making their cruelty complete.

It wasn't because she was naked in the pictures that she feared them. A body was just a body, after all, and she was certain that there were others out there far more interesting to look at than hers. It was the fact that they'd been taken without her knowledge; without her consent. She'd shown up for that audition with the hope and excitement she did for all of them. She'd not given the camera in the room a second thought—why would she? But then she'd woken up hours after sipping that bitter cup of coffee with no idea what had happened to her.

Those pictures were more than just a few titillating shots of a naïve young actress, they were evidence of her exploitation by people who wanted nothing but to humiliate her for profit.

Now she was counting on that weakness—the need to profit from her abuse—to save her. She wasn't their first victim; she'd learned that when she'd planned to go to the police. Others had fallen for the same fake audition, the same bitter cup of coffee, and their claims that they hadn't consented to the photos had been laughed at in blogs and magazines, by Twitter trolls and Facebook friends.

The one constructive thing Abby had learned was that the photos had only emerged when the women hit the big time. When they'd signed the contract on that summer blockbuster or become the face of a beauty brand. The photos had been squirreled away by their enterprising abusers; saved for when they could do the most damage. Fetch the highest possible price.

"I need to talk to you," Ethan said. "What are you doing working here, of all places? It's been almost impossible to find you. Is this some sort of research?"

"No, it's not bloody research, it's my life. Did it ever occur to you that there might be a reason why I'm so hard to find? That if I wanted to meet people I'd list a phone number, or an address, or retain an agent?"

Ethan stared at her, no doubt unused to such blatant rudeness, but it wasn't anger she saw in his eyes, it was something more dangerous. He was looking at her—really looking. Studying her features. Taking in every detail. His eyes had barely left her face since she'd dragged him into the alley, except the one time that they'd dropped to the hem of her skirt, down her legs, and back up again. Blood rushed to her face.

"I'm sorry, but I have nothing to say to you, and I don't think you could have anything to say that might interest me. Now, if you'll excuse me, I have to get back to work."

She had turned back towards the street when she heard him speak her name, his voice raised slightly, not in anger, but the tone of a man who is used to getting his own way. When she looked at him, the expression on his face confirmed that he had never had a woman, never mind an actress, walk away from him.

"Miss Richards, I am sorry to bother you at work," he said, without sounding the least bit sorry, "but I need to talk to you. If there's a problem with your boss, I can pay him for your time."

She walked back over to where he was standing and tried to keep her voice low, convinced that anyone passing in the street might be watching them.

"You don't understand. I can't talk to you. Not here. Not anywhere. I cannot be seen talking to you. I don't expect you to understand, but I do expect you to leave." She was angry at him for showing up here, but she was also terrified. He had to leave—right now. Because Ethan Walker drew publicity like a true A-lister. One innocent snap of a cameraphone could have her picture in the paper by tomorrow, and her gossip-value rising in the eyes of her attackers. But even as she was sending him daggers with her eyes, fighting him off with her body language, she could feel a very small, very rebellious part of her brain willing him to take no notice. Abby wondered if that part of her brain was having a bigger influence on her than she'd thought, because Ethan looked anything but put off. He smiled at her indulgently, his look of supreme confidence not slipping for a moment.

"Well, if you can't talk here, I'll send a car for you later. We can talk at my place. If you give me your address, I'll leave right now."

And if you don't, I'll cause a scene. He didn't have to say it aloud for Abby to hear the threat.

The winning hand. *He knows I'll do anything to get rid of him.* Part of her was impressed that he'd read the situation so quickly and calculated how best to get what he wanted. She couldn't afford to hesitate. She scribbled on her order pad, thrust the piece of paper into his hand, and walked away without looking back. He could send as many cars as he liked, it didn't mean she had any intention of getting into them. Hopefully then he would get the message.

Safely back inside the diner, she watched him walk to his car and she wished, more than just about anything, that she hadn't glanced at his backside. Because now she couldn't look away. Thank God he hadn't turned back to look at her; she was standing there like some seedy voyeur. It wasn't until she heard the car turn the corner at the end of the street that she walked back into the kitchen.

"And where did you disappear to? Apparently some guy walked in here and you took off with him?" Candy asked, eager for something to liven up their morning.

Despite her pin-up girl looks—she was taller than Abby by a good six inches, and had been blessed with perfect California-blonde hair and killer curves—Candy showed no interest in the Hollywood movie scene, which was why she was the only person Abby could currently count as a friend. But Abby knew how gossip and rumors could spread almost by accident—a casual remark, a careless comment—and trusting anyone with her secret was too great a risk.

Lying was second nature to her now, and she'd been working on her excuse from the minute she'd recognized Ethan. But just because it came easily to her, it didn't mean she had to enjoy it. Abby cringed inwardly as she spun Candy another story. "Oh, he's a friend of a friend back home. My friend told him I was living out here and he promised him that he'd call in and see how I'm doing. I didn't want to look like I was slacking, talking to a friend at work." Okay, she and Ethan had both worked in the same business. It wasn't completely impossible that they had a mutual acquaintance in London. Abby was pretty sure that this could be filed under stretching the truth rather than bare-faced lie.

"So, will you be seeing him again?"

"Oh, I doubt it. He was just doing his friend a favor really, looking in on me." It was fortunate she was a good actress. The last thing she needed was Candy knowing that, yes, ninety-nine percent of her brain was telling her that she never wanted to see him again, but that irritating one percent was getting louder by the minute. Especially now that the danger of Ethan being recognized had passed.

Anyway, she didn't think that he'd be that easy to shake. She'd seen the look in his eyes when she said she wouldn't talk to him. And not only did he look like he wouldn't be giving up on her, he didn't think he'd have to. He seemed sure—probably with good reason—that he could make anyone do exactly what he wanted just by asking them.

• • •

Ethan slowed the car to a stop and tried to work out what had just happened. It had taken him weeks to track Abby down to the diner. When he'd found the address and seen what neighborhood it was in, he hadn't believed it. In fact, he'd gone back and checked the information. Twice. But there she was. Working in a diner in the worst part of the city.

Before today he hadn't given much thought to why Abby was waiting tables. It wasn't like it was an unusual situation for an actress new to LA. True, from what he'd seen from her work in England, he hadn't expected that she would be short of roles. Her starring role in the UK's biggest soap opera had made her the nation's sweetheart. Most of the men in the country had fallen in love with her bright blue eyes, messy blonde curls, and innocent expression.

But the business out here could be pretty harsh. A sharp word or two in an audition, the suggestion that an actress might need to lose a little weight, have a little work done, were by no means unusual, and would knock the confidence of even the most seasoned professional.

Not that Abby needed any work, of course. Anyone who suggested it was an idiot. The girl was perfect. He thought back to the time he had first seen her face. Stuck in a hotel in London, flicking through cable channels to pass the time, he had come across reruns of a soap opera. Not the sort of thing that would usually catch his attention, but the screen was filled with this mesmeric face, and he found that he couldn't change the channel; didn't want to. The scenes she was in were lit up by her presence. Her talent would have been remarkable even without that face, that petite, elfin body, but all together as a package, she was perfect.

As soon as he'd seen Abby on TV, he'd known that he'd found his lead actress. He couldn't see anyone else holding a scene, speaking the words, like Abby would. The moment the credits had rolled on screen he'd called his assistant and given the details of the show.

"I want to see this girl before I go back to LA. Find her and set up a meeting."

When his assistant got back to tell him that he couldn't find her, he'd been furious, though of course hadn't shown it. He had personally called Abby Richards' agent and demanded that he send her for an audition immediately. But Marcus hadn't seen her for two years, not since she'd left England for LA. Ethan did some more digging—it seemed as if *no one* had seen her for two years. That was when he'd hired the detective.

Whatever was holding her back, Ethan could overcome it. He had to, because if he couldn't persuade her to make this movie, his career was as good as over. The script had been in preproduction for years, waiting for the right team to be put together. It had been rewritten endless times, and all the big-name directors had had their name attached to the project at some time or another. He had finally got the script just right; the team just right. Everything but the lead actress. Everyone he had auditioned and screen tested had been okay, some had even been excellent, but no one was perfect and now the financiers were talking about pulling out. If that happened, the movie would never get made, and it would be no one's fault but his own. Even if *rumors* about financial problems got out, it was ruined. Any threat of money trouble and people would start pulling out left, right, and center. The considerable financial stake he'd invested would be gone, but more importantly, his reputation would be ruined. He might never get another movie off the ground again.

He needed Abby. She had changed, yes, but the changes were all for the better as far as he was concerned. He doubted that many people would recognize her if they walked into the diner. He wasn't sure what it was—there was no disguise, no drastic change. It was more an accumulation of subtle changes; her hair slightly fairer, her skin glowing more. Most of all, she looked like the least vulnerable person he'd ever met. There was a fierceness in her eyes that hadn't been there on screen.

And she was beautiful. That first time he'd seen her on screen he'd been instantly attracted; his whole body had seemed to come alive when he saw her. He'd expected that after weeks of looking at her on screen—watching reruns and showreels—the effect would have weakened. But nothing had prepared him for how he felt when she'd dragged him down that alley. The way his arms had ached to pull her close to him. The spark of heat where she'd held his hand in hers.

Her reaction to him had been unexpected, admittedly. She hadn't just been uninterested, she'd been furious. Well, that might be a minor stumbling block, but nothing he couldn't handle. Once she knew what he was offering her, there was no way she could say no.

If he'd thought she was perfect for the role before he met her, he was certain of it now. She was enchanting. Utterly mesmerizing. And he had to have her.

Chapter Two

Abby stepped under the shower, letting the water sluice over her hair, washing out eight hours' worth of burger grease. She wasn't going to go. Ethan Walker was bad news and she wanted nothing to do with him. She had no interest in anything he had to say, so why would she bother going over to his place?

She didn't even want to think about why he might want to talk to her. Once upon a time she would have been intrigued; desperate to know. Was he going to ask her to audition for a part? That had to be it. Why else would a producer go to the effort of finding her? Whatever it was, it had to be serious.

She thought she'd made herself pretty much invisible. She used her legal name—Abigail Smith—not her stage name, Abby Richards. She lived a completely unremarkable, ordinary life; she kept herself away from anything or anyone that might provoke even a hint of curiosity about her past. As far as she knew, her boss, her landlord, Candy, and the tax man were the only people who knew her address.

But Ethan Walker, THE Ethan Walker, had found her, and when she'd tried to send him away, he had refused to take no for an answer. Surely this was it. This was her break. The moment that she'd dreamed of in the damp, dilapidated bedsit that she'd put up with because it was a stone's throw from her London drama school.

But that wasn't her dream anymore. Hollywood wasn't her dream. All she wanted now was to keep a low profile, to never see herself in a glossy magazine, and maybe one day—when the tabloids lost interest in her—go home to England. Drama school seemed like a different lifetime. She wasn't that person anymore. She couldn't let herself wonder what Ethan might want. And she absolutely could not go to his house tonight.

Unfortunately this message didn't seem to be getting through to her hands, which had just finished shaving her left shin. Bugger. Okay, so it wasn't like this meant anything. She didn't have to go just because she'd shaved her legs. That would patently be ridiculous. But the thought of Ethan's hands gliding up her now-silky-smooth calves ... Yesterday the thought of anyone's hands on her body would have made her feel...well, nothing at all. Not once since the day she'd woken up with her underwear on inside out, and hours missing from her memory, had she thought about sex for even a minute.

She'd gone to the doctor and told her what had happened with as little detail as possible—she had to know if anything had happened beyond the removal of her clothes. Needed to know what consequences she might be facing. She'd been overwhelmed with relief when she was told there was no sign of physical violation. But that didn't make her feel any less sickened. Any less determined that her attackers wouldn't add to her distress by publishing those photographs.

And she'd not touched a man since. Not out of any disgust or fear. It had just seemed that that part of her personality, the part that had enjoyed sex, loved intimacy, had disappeared. Being close enough to another person for either of those things to be possible was too much of a risk.

But she thought of how it had felt to have Ethan's hand in hers—how naturally she'd grabbed it, how she hadn't even realized she'd kept hold of it—and wondered what it was between them that made her feel comfortable, safe, even when she knew seeing Ethan Walker was anything but.

Perhaps she could go say "thank you very much, but no" to whatever it was he wanted to discuss, and enjoy surreptitiously looking at him for a few minutes. When was the last time she had spent any time with a man who wasn't in the process of stuffing his face with fries and soda? The clientele of the Hollywood Diner did not present many opportunities for ogling, and it wasn't like she had any intention of doing anything other than looking. Even the thought of an evening looking—just looking—at Ethan was making her tingle in places she'd forgotten she had.

But no, she had to be sensible. Smooth shins were a setback in her Get Rid of Ethan Walker plan, but it didn't matter because she wasn't going anyway.

This wasn't a game, she reminded herself. It was all good and well thinking about flirting with Ethan, and wondering whether he might be attracted to her. But she couldn't let her re-emerging libido cloud her mind. This wasn't real. Ethan Walker was Hollywood personified. He was danger personified. He was everything she'd been hiding from. More than with anyone else, a connection with Ethan Walker could blow her cover and bring her out into the open. One photograph of the two of them together, a little tabloid speculation, an overzealous intern determined to uncover the identity of "Ethan's Mystery Friend." That's all it would take to bring everything crashing down around her. She couldn't let a naughty twinkle in dark eyes and a tight backside blind her to the realities of her life. She couldn't go.

She tried to imagine Ethan's reaction when the car he sent for her returned empty. She had only spent a few minutes in his company, but it didn't take any longer than that to know that he was a man who expected, without doubt, to always get his own way. She was under no illusion that she was special to Ethan in some way, that he would desperately pursue her for her own sake, but he'd had a look in his eyes when she met him earlier that let her know that he never gave up once he'd locked on to his quarry. He'd make her keep her word, and do what he wanted—it would be a matter of pride.

So she would at least have to go out to the car. Perhaps she could give his driver a note to say that she wasn't coming. Would that be enough? No. She already knew that Ethan had planned this too carefully—the very fact that he'd taken the time and effort to track her down made that clear. He would make things difficult for her at work if she didn't do as he asked. He'd backed her into a corner, and despite all the precautions she'd taken, everything she'd sacrificed to keep herself protected, she had no way out.

The least bad option on offer was to go to Ethan's place, be absolutely clear that he could not contact her again, and make sure she left there on her own terms, without Ethan on her tail. Well, if she was going she was doing this her way, and she was giving Ethan absolutely no idea of the little fantasies that had played out in her mind that afternoon. She dried herself off from the shower and sat at the tiny table in her kitchen, makeup and mirror set out in front of her.

She kept the makeup minimal—the last thing she wanted was to look as if she'd made an effort—pulled the waves from her hair with her ancient hairdryer, and pinned it into a tight knot at the nape of her neck. Her clothes were formal and uninviting—severely cut grey trousers and a plain black jersey top. She didn't care that she wouldn't look out of place at a funeral. It suited her mood. To get through tonight she needed to be distant; cold. She was counting on Ethan getting the message and removing himself from her life.

When she looked in the mirror, Abby was pleased with the overall result. Whatever Ethan had seen in her that made him track her down, she was sure it was gone. If two years in deepest, darkest, dirtiest LA hadn't dragged it out of her, then she was sure this little makeover had. She checked her reflection in the mirror one last time and set her game face in place. Ethan Walker wouldn't stand a chance against the ice queen.

• • •

Abby sat in the car, her teeth worrying her ragged cuticles as she tried again to understand what she was doing there. *If I don't come tonight, he'll show up at work again,* Abby repeated to herself. True, Ethan probably would blow her cover if she didn't show up, but she couldn't help but remember that her initial reasons for wanting to come were not so wholesome. She suspected that when it came down to it, her presence in the car might have as much to do with Ethan's dark good looks as it had to do with protecting herself.

But she had her game plan, and as long as she stuck to it, she'd be fine. This wasn't so bad really. No real damage had been done. No one would see her talking to Ethan. All she had to do was find out what he wanted—and she had a feeling she already knew the answer to that—politely decline, and leave. There was nothing that he could do to change her mind about *this*, of that she was certain, so she just had to go, make her excuses, give him no hope that she would ever change her mind, and leave. Simple.

Except it didn't feel simple. She hadn't been able to stop thinking about Ethan since he'd left the diner that morning. She'd been distracted all day, and she knew that her story to Candy about never wanting to see him again wasn't going to hold.

It suddenly dawned on her that she had no idea where the car was taking her. She drew in a jagged breath. How could she have been so stupid? Had she learned nothing? She'd just stepped into a strange man's car with no idea where it was taking her, and no one knew where she was. She'd flat out denied to Candy that she was going anywhere tonight. If anything happened to her no one would even know about it until she failed to show up for work tomorrow, and by then it could be too late. She knew that she was probably overreacting, but instinctive fear gripped her, and she pulled her mobile out of her bag.

Am meeting the friend of friend tonight for drink. Will call you later for debrief. Call me if I don't call you.

As soon as she'd worked out where she was she'd text Candy again and let her know. Not ideal, but the best she could do with the situation she'd put herself in.

She could see that Thomas, the driver, kept checking on her in the rearview mirror. She must look as stressed out as she felt. Or had he heard her panicked scrabbling, trying to find her phone in her bag? She suspected he knew that something wasn't quite right from how many times he looked back at her. At one point she was sure that he was going to say something, but he seemed to think the better of it and his mouth remained closed. Had he driven other nervous young women to Ethan's house? She didn't even want to think about that…

The car slowed and she looked out of the window to try and see where she was. From the view of the lights she guessed she must be somewhere up in Beverly Hills. From way up here she could see the city stretched out for miles around her, and she knew that she was entering silly-money territory.

These kinds of views didn't come cheap, and from the occasional glance she got of the houses behind eight-foot-high gates, this was home to Hollywood royalty. Holed up in their obscenely large and extremely gaudy mansions, way out of the reach of the masses.

Acting had never been about the money for her. She had never been interested in the showbiz side of the business, she just wanted to act. It was all she could ever remember wanting to do. Now that that dream was over, she couldn't help feel that those who had been lucky enough to get their opportunity, and smart enough not to throw it away, had had their heads turned by the money and the glamour.

She wouldn't be able to afford a house around here if she saved for a million years. Not that she would want to even if she could, she reminded herself. This sort of ostentatious wealth was never something she desired. She wondered how many of the people in the houses around her really appreciated what they had, and whether they knew how perhaps, with one stupid mistake, they too could end up waitressing in a dingy diner.

There was more money than sense around here, and in places certainly more money than taste. She had no doubts that Ethan's place would be the same. A gilded trophy of a house, built and bought with the purpose of showcasing wealth. She knew that she sounded bitter, but she couldn't help but resent those who wasted their success on marble-lined pool houses.

She checked her watch again. It felt as if she had been in the car for hours, but it hadn't been much more than forty minutes. She thought again about what she would say to Ethan. How she would make him understand that whatever it was he wanted to ask her, the answer would have to be no. Whatever Ethan Walker wanted, she couldn't be a part of it. After today, she could never see him again.

She felt a clench in her stomach at that thought. Traitor. Despite everything, the attraction that she felt for him still threatened to overwhelm her better judgment, but it wouldn't. It couldn't. She just had to tell him no, and then walk away.

The car slowed as a pair of enormous automatic gates opened. Despite their size, they were more discreet than Abby had been expecting, certainly not as gaudy as some of the others that she had seen on the drive over here. She was fully prepared—hoping even—to hate Ethan Walker's house, but as the car rounded a corner of the driveway she knew that she had got this one wrong. It was a mansion alright, there was no getting away from the size of the thing, or the fact that it must have cost ten, twenty, a hundred times what a normal family home might cost, but it was beautiful. Damn him. It would be so much easier to remember not to be nice to him if he had terrible taste; if he loved all the things that she despised. But she had the feeling that the inside of this house would be as beautiful, and as tasteful, as the exterior.

She stood from the car, and felt the contents of her handbag spill from her lap onto the gravel drive. She scrabbled, trying desperately to gather up tampons, lip glosses, and old receipts before Thomas, or—God forbid—Ethan, should feel the need to come to her aid. Luckily, Thomas seemed to sense her discomfort and kept his distance, and there was no sign of Ethan from behind the huge oak front door. With everything safely zipped back inside her handbag, she walked towards the door. Thomas seemed to have slipped away, and she faltered. Should she knock? Ring the bell?

She was saved from her indecision when the door was flung open in front of her, and there Ethan stood, in the same jeans and now slightly crumpled white shirt he had worn to the diner. The only change to his outfit, as far as she could see, was his bare feet. She refused to be thrilled by a feeling of intimacy. She watched as Ethan looked her up and down, and tried to gauge his reaction to her appearance. But he was giving nothing away.

Once she could drag her eyes away from Ethan, she looked past him into the entrance hall, and instantly realized how wrong she had been about his lifestyle. There was no inlaid monographed marble and not a lick of gold leaf in sight. She instantly felt annoyed, though at herself or at Ethan she couldn't decide. Ethan had wrong-footed her again, but only because she had been so quick to judge him. She had just assumed that he would be crass and tacky—not that he had ever done anything that might have hinted at it. She only had herself to blame for jumping to conclusions.

"Abby, welcome."

"It's Abigail." With her own body rebelling against her protective instincts, Abby knew the only way to keep herself safe from Ethan was to play the ice queen. She couldn't, even for a second, let him know that she wanted anything but to get away from here as soon as possible. But even in the face of her icy tones and bad manners, Ethan was—infuriatingly—the embodiment of hospitality as he led her through to the kitchen and offered her a drink.

The house was stylish and sophisticated, neither the gaudy, gold leaf-adorned crib, nor the plasma TV and black leather bachelor pad she had imagined. But although it was beautiful, she could see nothing of Ethan in it. She couldn't imagine him choosing the curtains or the scatter cushions. If she had to guess, then she'd say that most of the rooms she glanced into hadn't been touched, never mind used, since the interior designer left the building. She wondered where Ethan really lived, because it certainly wasn't in the parts of the house she had seen so far.

The kitchen seemed a little more homely than the rest of the house, though that might have had something to do with the incredible smell coming from the stove. She looked around, wondering where the army of staff it must take to maintain an estate like this were lurking. *I bet they're used to being discrete, though,* Abby thought, wondering how many women had been picked up and brought here like this, and how many had stayed until the next morning. Ethan was LA's most eligible bachelor, and if his past was anything to go by, also the least likely to be taking himself off the market any time soon.

• • •

"It's just us this evening." Ethan couldn't take his eyes off her face. She looked worried, her eyes darting towards the door every few seconds, as if she was worried the kitchen would be stormed any second. He figured she was worried about people seeing her here, remembering what she had said at the diner. Why was she so nervous, he wondered. He was used to women getting a little tongue tied around him, it came with the job title, but this was different. She'd scraped back her hair in a style as severe as her expression, and for the first time he wondered whether this evening might be more difficult than he had initially anticipated. Behind her icy glare, he could see that she was scared—terrified even—and he had no idea why, or what he could do about it. All he knew was that something told him he'd never be satisfied with doing nothing. He needed to find out what was paining her; he needed to fix it. "I hope that's okay. And you don't need to worry about Thomas. He's very discreet. Wine?" Ethan offered, gesturing to the rack on the kitchen counter.

"Thanks."

This would be a long night if she planned on communicating entirely in monosyllables. Longer still if he couldn't get his body under control. Every time he looked at her, he had to stop himself from reaching out and touching her. Every time her eyes shot to the door, and the fear flickered in her eyes, he wanted to pull her into his arms, protect her from whatever had her so frightened. It was nothing, he told himself. It was just that he had been looking for her for so long, had thought of her face every day, that the lines between business and pleasure had started to blur. Yes, he wanted her, but he wanted her for his movie. Okay, he might not say no to taking both, if the opportunity arose, but his priorities here were clear.

Abby leaned back against the kitchen counter as Ethan poured them each a glass of red wine. "I think maybe we got off on the wrong foot before." He decided to tread lightly; go with the charm offensive; soothe her. Maybe she would loosen up a bit if he showed her she had nothing to fear from him. It was only a short step from there to her agreeing to tell him what was holding her back, and then taking the part he was offering. And he needed her to agree. "And I am sorry for coming to you at work, but it was the only way that I could find to get hold of you."

"How did you find me?" Well, at least monosyllables meant getting to the point.

"Well, to be honest, I'm not sure I can answer that. It wasn't me personally who found you. I hired a detective."

"You hired someone to follow me?" Her blue eyes grew wider and he wondered what she was hiding…or hiding from. Because the more she said, or didn't say, the more he was sure she was keeping something secret. Something big.

She took the glass of wine that Ethan held out to her, and sat when he moved towards the sofa at the far end of the kitchen, tucking her petite frame into the corner of the couch, but she wouldn't meet his eyes when he leaned against the counter opposite her.

"Not to follow you, to find you," he clarified. "Two completely different things as far as I'm concerned." She was making him out to be some kind of stalker. That wasn't it at all. He had this amazing opportunity for her, so why was she making it so difficult? "To be honest, this isn't the reaction I was expecting."

"No, I don't suppose it is."

Her face was truly fascinating, he thought, even as she seemed to be getting angrier by the second. Her cheekbones and nose were so delicate they were almost ethereal, creating a striking contrast with the hard, angry lines she was pulling her forehead and mouth into. He shook his head and reminded himself that this was work. He had to focus on the task at hand.

"I just thought you might be more interested in why I tracked you down, rather than how."

"Well spit it out then. Why did you have me stalked? Because whatever the reason I can promise you it's been a waste of time and money."

"I want to offer you a part in a movie." He waited for her to smile, to thank him, to agree. Surely if anything was going to cure her antagonism it would be this.

"Is this the part where I'm meant to swoon?"

Perhaps not.

That wasn't meant to happen. Actresses normally promised the world—with every intention of delivering—to get a part in one of his movies. And now the one girl he really wanted—no, needed—was turning him down?

He wasn't used to being taken by surprise, and the unfamiliar sensation of a situation moving out of control was far from welcome. But this was only a minor setback, he reminded himself. She could be persuaded; he was sure. "Don't you want to know a little bit about the part?"

"No thanks. I'm not interested in acting, or the movie business, anymore, so it doesn't matter what the part is. I'm sorry for the trouble you've gone through." She didn't look sorry in the slightest as she stood up from the couch. "Now I just need to call a taxi and then I'll be out of your way." She still looked angry, and he knew that getting her more riled up wasn't going to get him anywhere. He just had to keep his eye on the goal—play it cool.

"Okay, I'm sorry you're not interested, I think you'd love the movie. But there's no need to rush off. Stay anyway." He softened his eyes as he smiled at her; a little old-fashioned charm surely couldn't hurt his chances. "There's a mountain of food, and I'm enjoying talking to you. I'd like to get to know you better…"

"That's kind," she replied, her eyes darting to the door, "but I've taken up enough of your time already. I really should be—" She was cut short by a rumble of thunder that seemed to emanate from her belly.

"That settles it." Ethan laughed, glad to have a legitimate reason to make her stay. "You're obviously starving. You'll stay for dinner." He could see she was still weighing up her options, but clearly deciding that arguing wasn't going to help. And she was right.

Ethan set the table in the kitchen for two and topped up Abby's wine.

"So, how long have you been working at the Hollywood Diner?"

It seemed like an innocent enough question, but her reaction was immediate. Her fingers clutched at her cutlery, and her hands started to shake. He watched, impressed, as she caught the rise of panic and forced it down.

"I've been there about two years." Okay, so she wasn't exactly offering stimulating conversation, and he could hear the slight shake in her voice, but at least it was approaching normal. If he could just ask the right questions, get to the bottom of what was holding her back, he knew he could fix this situation, and in the process, make whatever it was that made her so wary of him go away. Because sitting looking at her panicking, he was suddenly struck with the thought that that was what he wanted. He wanted to see her smile, to laugh, to relax—with him. *So she can make the film,* he reasoned. Because if he could make her happy, she could make the film.

"So you must have started there just after you moved to California." He carried on pushing the conversation forwards, despite her resistance. Her head snapped up as the death grip returned. His arm twitched, ready to reach out and take her hand, to stoke her fingers with his until she calmed. He forced it back to his side, knowing instinctively that to try and touch her now would spook her.

"It seems like your investigator did a thorough job," she replied through gritted teeth, her voice full of ice. "Why ask questions that you already know the answer to?" Her white knuckles were still shaking, and he watched as she managed to pry her fingers off her cutlery and place her hands under the table.

"Actually, not as good a job as I'd hoped," Ethan replied. "He managed to find out when you came to the States, where you stayed, and people you met with for the first couple of days, and then nothing. It was as if you had disappeared. He found it quite frustrating actually." He felt uncomfortable, pushing her, when she obviously didn't want to talk about it, but he was sure that he was on the right track. And if she'd just tell him what was the problem, then he could take care of it.

"And did you not think that if someone has gone to the effort of not being found, then maybe they just want to be left alone?"

"Ah, so you do admit that you were deliberately hiding."

"In my experience, if someone goes to great lengths not to be found, there is a reason for it."

"What happened?" He barely recognized his voice, so low and soft, but he couldn't help it. He could see that she was traumatized, and it was killing him to just sit there and not help. He wanted to pull her from her seat into his arms until that haunted look left her face. *This has to stop*, he chastised himself. This was business. He would do what he needed to help her, so that his entire professional life didn't go under.

"I decided that acting wasn't for me after all, that's all. Hollywood wasn't what I was expecting. I changed my mind."

She was lying to him. He didn't know why, but he was absolutely certain there had to be more to it than that.

"But you decided to stay in LA?"

"Oh, my mother…we seem to get along better when I'm five thousand miles away." And she didn't need a visa—she'd secured US citizenship when she was still a teenager, his investigator had found that much out—her father was American, though he'd moved to the UK after college.

"So the fact that the movie's being shot in England isn't going to help persuade you?"

"Not in the slightest."

He kept his eyes on her face, trying to see any clues to what was really going on here. His eyes came to rest on her plump bottom lip. No answers there, but still he found it difficult to drag his eyes away.

This was not what he had been expecting. He was used to calling the shots, being in control. He knew if a woman was interested in him, professionally or otherwise, and knew how to make sure they both got what they wanted. He wasn't used to being so utterly in the dark. It was clear from her manner and her appearance that she was trying to keep him at a distance. The question was why.

But he had to face facts—right now he was more interested in her than she was in him. He needed her more than she needed him. But he was sure that he could win her over. If he could just find out what was behind her reluctance, the reasons for the hostile defenses that greeted him at every turn, he was sure he could persuade her. He was yet to meet any woman, any*one*, in fact, who could resist him for long.

Chapter Three

"So, thanks for dinner, but I should really be going." Abby had checked her watch three times in the last fifteen minutes but so far her subtle hints didn't seem to be working. Either Ethan hadn't noticed or he was deliberately ignoring her. Either way, Abby had had enough. "Could you tell me your address? I'll need to give it to the taxi company." The taxi would just about bankrupt her, but it would be worth it to get out of here. This evening hadn't panned out as she'd hoped. She'd thought that she'd be able to say a polite but firm "no" to Ethan, spend a couple of minutes committing that face to memory, and then be on her way. She hadn't been prepared for his questions or his concern.

He'd had her on edge all night, so much she'd almost been able to forget what she'd been thinking in the shower earlier, forget that she'd imagined Ethan's hand smoothing its way up her shin, her thigh, higher ... She caught the thought before it fully formed.

"Don't worry about a cab, I'll drive you home."

She hadn't seen that one coming. As soon as he said the words she could feel the panic starting to rise again. He wasn't going to make it easy for her to walk away. But every minute she spent with him felt like it was bringing her closer to ruin. Letting this connection between them grow—indulging herself, enjoying his company—could only lead to disaster. She reminded herself what was at stake. If she didn't cut this off now, then those photos could be in the hands of some journalist within hours; minutes. And then anyone who wanted to could see her spread naked, vulnerable, molested, and her violation would be complete.

But how was she supposed to manage this situation if Ethan contradicted her at every turn? All she had to do was keep this simple, and insist a taxi was fine. How hard could that be?

She took a deep breath and steadied herself, trying to keep her voice level. "Thank you, but you really don't have to do that. If you could just tell me your address, I'll get a taxi here in a few minutes. Besides, you've been drinking."

Except he hadn't. She only now noticed that the glass of red wine he'd poured for himself was untouched. He'd topped up his water glass, and her wine glass, a couple of times, but hadn't had a sip of the wine. *Recovering alcoholic?* she wondered. *Control freak, more like.* Because if he didn't drink, then he could insist on driving her home. All part of his grand plan. Well, she'd come here to listen to his offer and give a polite refusal. He may be gorgeous, almost to the point of distraction, but she wasn't here to be toyed with. She would not be manipulated.

"Why won't you tell me your address?"

"It's not that I won't give you my address—"

"But you haven't."

"No, I haven't, because there's no need. I'll drive you home."

"Why won't you just give me your address? Are you planning on keeping me prisoner here, is that what's happening?" It was a good thing she was an actress. Even as she was saying the words she could hear how melodramatic they sounded. A lesser woman would have given herself the giggles. But Abby needed to get herself out of this house now, to get away from him, and if this was what it took, then so be it.

She saw a frown flicker across his features before he smoothed it into his usual professional, charming grin. At last, a reaction. He had slipped and she knew that underneath his cool façade he was starting to crack from the pressure of her ice queen routine. She was fairly sure that he knew she wasn't serious, but she didn't imagine it was much fun to be accused of false imprisonment all the same. She wished that this wasn't necessary, that it wasn't so imperative that she leave. There was part of her—a startlingly loud part—that wanted to settle into this house and never go. And it wasn't the furnishings that were attracting her.

As she faced Ethan across the table, trying to provoke him into reacting with a steely glare, she wondered how this might have turned out if this had all happened when she had first arrived in LA. She would have jumped at Ethan's offer of a part, but would she have still ended up sharing dinner in his home? If she had, she was pretty sure that she wouldn't be trying to provoke him into throwing her out.

There was no point denying that she was attracted to Ethan. The man was gorgeous. Any woman could tell you that. More than once over dinner she'd found herself trying to decide the exact color of his eyes—they were a deep, dark brown, but were there other colors in there too? A hint of chocolate, a flash of gold…or work out how the fine lines around them made him *more* attractive. The man even made wrinkles look good.

But there was something else drawing her to him. His supreme confidence that he would get his own way bordered on arrogance; his insistence on getting what he wanted was infuriating, but somehow she knew that he would be less attractive without it. Here was a man who knew what he wanted, and would fight to get it. All the more reason to get out of here. The only way she'd had to protect herself over the past two years was by keeping a firm control on who she let into her life. She couldn't afford any sort of association with someone who might lead her to exposure.

Ethan's face hinted at a smirk.

"Don't be silly, of course you're free to leave any time you like. It's just I'd rather drive you myself, that way I know you're home safely."

"I appreciate your concern. But really, I'm an adult, and I'm perfectly capable of worrying about my own safety. I'd like your address please."

"No."

"Just 'no'?"

"I told you, I'm driving you home. You have no good reason to turn down my kind offer, so I'll bring the car round and wait for you out front."

Abby scrabbled around in her brain for anything that might change his mind. "I don't want you to know where I live," she blurted. When it came to keeping her distance, this was fundamental, after all.

"Why not?" A reasonable enough question, she supposed.

"Because I think you might be serious about wanting to offer me this part, and if this discussion's anything to go by, you're a little too used to getting your own way. If you knew where I lived, you might be tempted to come round and persuade me. A lot. I don't want that."

"Thomas picked you up this evening; you've already given me your address."

"That wasn't my address."

"What?" Again, it was just a flicker around the jawline, but enough to let her know he wasn't happy to have been outwitted.

"Like I said, that wasn't my address; I just chose a place for him to pick me up. I was waiting at the pavement."

She saw Ethan take a moment to absorb this information and reassess his opponent; he obviously hadn't realized she was taking this so seriously. He brought out his counterattack; no doubt part of a carefully thought-out plan that he was certain would get him what he wanted. "Well, you're forgetting that I already know where you work. What if I try to come and persuade you there?"

Far from becoming more aggressive at her insistence, his voice slipped into an altogether smoother tone, no doubt honed on many women before her. If she didn't know better, she'd say that he was starting to flirt. She guessed he was a pro. Right at this minute, she wanted nothing more than Ethan to *persuade* her into a dozen different things. But flirting was just another trick in his arsenal. Another tactic for getting what he wanted. No doubt he had good reason to have faith in his skills, but unlike most women he met, she had strong motivation to resist. Flirting with Ethan Walker could lead to nothing but disaster.

It didn't matter how attracted she was to him. It didn't even matter if he was attracted to her. The fact of the matter was that after today she could never see him again. Even if his flirting was genuine, a mutual attraction would make that more important, not less. She had to find a way to get him out of her life.

"Simple. At work, if you upset me, my friend throws you out."

"You're sure about that?" The sparkle in his eyes and suggestive lilt to his voice told her she was right. He was going to try and flirt his way out of this one.

"Very sure. She didn't take kindly to you bothering me earlier." No harm in a little white lie. Lying was just a necessary, if unpleasant, part of her life these days.

"She noticed?"

"Eyes like a hawk." When it came down to it she was sure that any of her colleagues at the diner, and a fair few of the regulars, would come to her rescue if they thought she needed it. But if that were necessary, then the chances of her past staying there were not good.

"I'm sorry."

It was the last thing that she expected to hear. Not only was the great Ethan Walker apologizing, but the look on his face told her that it was genuine. She could tell he knew how important it was for her that her past stayed a secret at work. *But that didn't stop him threatening to visit,* she reminded herself.

"But there's no one to kick me out if I hassle you at home?" She had to admire his quick thinking and change of subject, but his question knocked his flirting up another level.

"No. There's just me." Abby almost didn't recognize her voice when she spoke, and she could have kicked herself for the sultry tone it had taken on. It was not what she had wanted, but from the look in Ethan's eyes, it had made quite an impression. Abby found that once her eyes had met Ethan's, she couldn't look away.

An attraction to Ethan could only lead to disaster, she reminded herself. It was easier to remember this when they had been talking about work; her career. But from the way he was looking at her now, she knew that the attraction wasn't one sided. It really was time she was home. It didn't matter how she got there, but spending more time with Ethan was a bad idea. Half an hour with him in the car while he was focused on driving would be a small price to pay to get out of here and back to the safety of her own home.

"Okay, you can drive me home."

• • •

As she'd suspected it might be, the car journey was agony. Ethan's flirting had created tension, and in the close confines of his car it was growing to be unbearable. Abby stared out the window, wondering whether she should turn the radio on. Ethan hadn't said a word since they'd pulled out of his driveway, and the awkward silence was gnawing away at her. Was he doing this so that she'd crack and say she'd be in his movie? So that she'd say anything to break the silence?

She was counting off the cross streets in her head, knowing with each one that she was that little bit closer to home; closer to safety. But part of her didn't want to get there. Here, in the car, she could almost pretend that this was real. That this had been a date, or at least a precursor to a date, and that something might be about to happen between them. She knew that as soon as she got out of his car the illusion would be shattered, and she would have to reinstate the distance between them. Back to reality.

She also knew that if the past few hours were anything to go by, then Ethan may well have other tricks up his sleeve to try and get her to agree to his movie. She decided that the best way to handle him was to make him think he was getting his own way. Bite her tongue a little now, and then get him out of her life for good.

She suppressed a sigh as they pulled up outside her apartment building.

She had never really grown to think of this place as home. It was difficult to feel that way about what passed for an apartment in this part of LA. The dusty streets still looked alien to the girl who had grown up in rural Surrey. Even after two years here, she couldn't get over the amount of space in this city. Even in the dodgiest neighborhoods the streets stretched straight ahead for miles. Burnt-out cars sat on pavements outside tired looking strip malls. And even the dirtiest, most suspect-looking houses occupied a plot bigger than a London family home. Her building had bars on the windows, half a dozen locks on the door, and a seedy character hanging around outside. What more could a girl ask for? But it was close to work, and let's face it—it was all she could afford.

"This is me," she told Ethan, and he pulled up behind an ambulance parked at the roadside. *What must he think*, Abby wondered; before reminding herself, *It doesn't matter what he thinks*. He was the one who had insisted on driving her home—he could hardly be rude about the apartment that she didn't want him to see in the first place. But from the way he was still holding onto the steering wheel, she knew that he wasn't happy about leaving her here. Well, he didn't have to be happy, he just had to go. She grabbed her handbag and reached for the door handle.

"This is the right place?" Ethan asked, trying to see around the ambulance and down the rest of the street.

"Yep, this is me." She could tell that he wasn't buying her forced brightness, but what did she care.

"Wait there. Do *not* open the door."

Abby let out a hiss of exasperation. This was *her* neighborhood. They were outside *her* apartment. What made him think that he could order her around, decide what was safe and what wasn't? But, Abby reminded herself, cooperation was going to be the best way to get him out of her hair as quickly as possible, and so she did as he asked and stayed in her seat until he came around the car and opened the door. Maybe he was just being a gentleman, she reasoned, no harm in that. But of course that wasn't it. He was trying to protect her. Sweet, perhaps, but she really didn't need—or *want*—his protection.

They walked in silence to the door of the building.

"Thanks for the lift…"

"I'm not letting you out of my sight until I know you're safe in your apartment."

How was she meant to keep her distance when he was so determined to barge his way into her life? She was about to argue when she remembered her decision. Cooperation. As long as he wasn't planning on coming any closer than her front door. "Have it your way…" She led the way into the building and started to climb the stairs. "I'm upstairs, are you still sure you want to see me all the way home?"

"You don't get rid of me that easily." *You don't get your own way that easily,* he might have said. Maybe not. But it was worth a try.

As Abby stepped out onto her landing, the door to one of the apartments slammed open. She hadn't given the ambulance outside much thought—it's not like it was an unusual sight for her neighborhood on a Saturday night—until she saw it was the door to her neighbor's apartment that had opened. Walking faster now, Abby headed along the hallway, wanting to check that her neighbor was okay. Her baby wasn't due for a couple of weeks, but perhaps it had decided to arrive a little earlier than planned.

The sounds coming from inside the apartment made Abby worry more; it didn't sound like all was well in there. She was almost at the door when a team of paramedics raced into the corridor carrying her neighbor, Marion, on a stretcher, forcing Ethan and Abby into a recess in the wall. Abby pressed herself back as far back as she could, hoping that they'd got out of the way quickly enough. Whatever had happened, it didn't look good, and she was sure that every second would count.

As the noise from the paramedics receded, Abby became aware of how tiny a space she and Ethan had squeezed themselves into. He'd braced his hands on either side of her head, and she could feel the length of his body pressing against hers. In the confines of the alcove, her breathing sounded unnaturally loud. Had Ethan noticed? She flicked her eyes up to his face, but only got as far as his lips, staring at them a fraction too long before quickly looking away.

You should not be looking at him like that, she told herself. *Those lips are strictly off limits.*

But her eyes flicked up again. Was she seeing things, or were they a little closer? They were definitely moving towards her. And in that moment she knew Ethan was going to kiss her. She moved her hands from where they'd been squeezed behind her back and placed them on Ethan's chest. Any minute, any second now, she was going to push him away. But her hands didn't seem to be moving—her mouth did. Her eyes closed, and she waited to feel Ethan's lips on hers.

"Ahem."

There they were; she knew they must have been there all along. Abby found her hands and firmly pushed. Ethan stepped away and she was presented with the sight of a policeman stepping out of her neighbor's apartment. The memory that she was hurt came flooding back, and Abby was embarrassed that she had been so easily distracted from her concern.

"Can you tell me what's happened? Is she okay?"

"Sorry, miss, but you shouldn't really be up here, this is a crime scene."

"I...I live here," she said, walking towards her front door, "and I just wanted to check whether Marion was okay. I know the baby's due very soon..."

"I'm afraid she's been shot, ma'am. It seems as if a stray bullet passed through the window. I'm sorry, but that's all we know right now."

Abby felt herself pale. A pregnant woman, shot in her own home. She had become pretty hardened to the violence and crime that was rife in her neighborhood, but this was something else. She slumped back against her door.

Until she felt him prizing the keys out of her hand, she had forgotten that Ethan was there. Without a word he unlocked her door and maneuvered her inside. She allowed herself to be led over to the couch and pressed down into the cushions. Ethan stood over her, his concern for her occupying every line of his face.

"Are you okay, Abby? Was—is—she a friend of yours?"

"Not a friend really." Abby took a breath and forced back tears. "I only know her to say hello to in the corridor, but I still can't believe it. Who could do something like that...?"

Ethan crouched down in front of her, holding her hand.

"I know it's really awful, and I hope that she and the baby are okay, but I'm sure she is being well cared for. Right now I'm more concerned about you. You can't stay here tonight."

That was enough to snap her out of her shock.

"What do you mean I can't stay here? It's my home; where else would I stay?"

Truth be told, the thought of sleeping here tonight wasn't exactly appealing. Knowing that it could just as easily have been her who got in the way of a stray bullet was terrifying. She didn't even know whether anyone had been arrested for the crime. But where else could she go? It wasn't like she had options—a hotel was out of the question on her wages. She supposed she could call Candy, but she only rented a single room with barely enough space for one.

"You'll stay with me, of course." Ethan was already standing, looking around as if he would start packing for her, so sure was he that Abby would go along with him.

Chapter Four

"Don't be ridiculous. I'm not staying with you."

Now *normally* the offer to stay in a Beverly Hills mansion wasn't something women turned down—not that he was given to making invitations often. But the scowl she sent in his direction made her feelings clear. So much for fantasy picking up from where that not-quite-kiss had left off.

He kept his expression level, not wanting to spook her into pushing him further away. There was no question that he was leaving her here—she would see that soon enough. The thought of something happening to her—something else bad, because she had obviously already been hurt—caused the uncomfortable feeling in his chest to return. He refused to consider the other reasons he might want her in his house: the attraction that was becoming harder to ignore, the kiss that had almost happened out in the corridor, and tried to be pragmatic.

"Look, this is very simple. I am not leaving this building without you. If you want me to drive you to a friend's house, fine. But from the look on your face, I don't think you have anywhere to go. So you're staying with me."

"I'll get a room in a hotel; it's only for a night or two."

He looked around her room. "You can't afford it."

Apparently that was going too far. He watched her eyebrows knit together and color rush to her face. He wanted to smooth away those lines, erase the worries that caused them, but the fierce expression in her eyes warned him not to try getting any closer.

"What I can and can't afford is none of your business." She hissed at him, clearly furious. But it wasn't his fault that he was the only one making sensible suggestions here.

"It is my business if I leave you here and you get hurt." He tried to make his voice reasonable, but gave her no doubt that this was not negotiable. He saw her fight down tears again and he wanted to reach out and comfort her.

His tone softened. Making her angrier would get him nowhere. "I know we haven't exactly gotten off to the best of starts, and I know you're angry at me. I promise you I don't mean to cause you any trouble. But all of that aside, you're not safe here, and you will be at my house. I can promise you that it's just the offer of a guest room, no strings attached—movie related, or…otherwise."

Abby raised an eyebrow at the last word. He didn't know what had made him say that, maybe the fact that seeing her here like this and not being able to drag her into his arms was making that strange feeling worse. He was certain that it was something he should stay well away from, and equally certain he wanted to explore it more. But he had to keep his head. Mixing business and pleasure was never easy and the movie had to come first.

"I…" He waited for her to try and think of an excuse. There was no excuse. A woman had just been shot six feet from Abby's front door and she had been offered a safe place to stay. He knew that she was lying about the hotel. Anywhere she went, he'd just track her down there anyway. "Thank you."

Trying not to gloat at his victory, but failing, Ethan went into action mode. "So, pack a bag and bring everything you need. It might take a while before you want to come back here, or before you can find somewhere else. What can I pack for you?"

She smiled at him. "Err, maybe you should just make us a coffee while I pack. I'll try and be as quick as I can."

• • •

Back in the car, sitting so close that Abby could smell a faint hint of Ethan's shower gel, she wondered—again—what on earth she was doing going to Ethan Walker's house. On the way to her apartment, the tension in the car had been kept to a just-about-bearable degree due to the knowledge that their close proximity would end shortly, and she would never have to see Ethan again. But now, driving away from what used to be her safe haven, there was no immediate end in sight. She pulled out her phone and fired another text message off to Candy telling her not to call, and that she'd explain everything to her in the morning.

As they pulled through the gates of Ethan's house, Abby sighed. This was not at all what she had planned for this evening. On the drive over she'd had to consider how she was going to get to work in the morning, and she was yet to come up with a good solution. Work was twenty miles away, her car was in the shop, and it would take hours to get there by public transport. It was looking increasingly likely that she would have to take a day or two's holiday if she was going to stay at Ethan's.

Ethan had jumped out of the car and pulled her bags out from the boot before she could get there herself. It was clear to Abby that if she was going to stay here, even if it was just for a night or two, she would have to lay down some ground rules, and soon. Her "cooperation" plan was starting to look like a seriously bad idea. She'd set a dangerous precedent just by agreeing to come here, and that would have to change.

As she approached the enormous front door she half expected it to be opened by an elderly butler or housekeeper—opening one's own front door seemed incongruous with a house on this scale, but then she remembered that Ethan had said earlier they were alone in the house—he must have given the staff the night off. She wondered again how many staff it took to maintain a house this size. She already knew that he had a driver, and she was certain that there would be at least a housekeeper and a gardener. How many other people would know that she was staying here? Should she have a word with Ethan, remind him how important her privacy was, how important it was that no one found out that she was here?

But surely that would lead to questions—questions that she wouldn't and couldn't answer.

"I'll show you up to a guest suite in a minute and let you get settled in. You must be wiped out."

Guest *suite*? Okay, so this wasn't exactly the ideal situation for someone trying to keep a low—well, invisible—profile. But it beat wandering aimlessly around LA, and it would have its perks.

"You didn't get the proper guided tour earlier, so let me quickly show you around now … Down here we have the kitchen, which you've seen, the dining room…" which would seat at least twenty and looked like it was rarely used, "…the living room…" artfully placed, uncomfortable looking furniture, "…the library is at the end of the hall and the cinema…" cinema! "…is off to the right."

So far the house was everything Abby had expected—beautiful, immaculately decorated, and furnished. Every room was a master class in luxurious neutrals, clean lines, lush fabrics. Vast white sofas and uncomfortable looking chairs were complemented by silk cushions, echoing the colors of the sky and the ocean. Despite the beauty of the rooms, Abby couldn't help but feel that there was something lacking. Something that neither a world-class designer nor priceless piece of art could provide: heart.

The house was beautiful. It was show-home perfect. But it was *too* beautiful. She could see no sign of Ethan here. No sign that these rooms were for anything but show. Aside from the kitchen, where they'd eaten earlier, it all looked decidedly…sterile. As if the cushions on the sofas and the books in the library hadn't moved since the interior designer had so carefully positioned them there.

In a corner of the grand entrance hall, Ethan led them through a door so discreet that Abby assumed it would take them through to the staff quarters.

"But here's where I really live."

Abby could see at once that no interior decorator had set foot in here for a long time. Not that there was anything wrong with the décor, though it was humble compared to the grand rooms she had seen so far. But whereas the rest of the house seemed cold and impersonal, all whites and creams, broken only occasionally with a hint of blue or green, these rooms were warm; welcoming. Laid-back, low-key, but still completely gorgeous. In Ethan's den the throw over the back of the battered brown leather couch was rumpled and DVDs were stacked on the floor in front of the enormous TV screen. Scripts and DVDs were piled everywhere, overspill from the study next door, where Ethan's heavy, old-fashioned desk was lost beneath yet more DVDs, piles of books, and other papers.

"You'll have to excuse the mess, I would say that it doesn't normally look like this but it wouldn't exactly be truthful."

"There's no need to apologize to me," Abby replied honestly. "I'm the one imposing on you." Whether she wanted to or not.

"Well, it's not like I don't like the rest of the house; it's beautiful, and people expect that sort of thing, but it's not really me. I much prefer to be back here. Plus, it's close to the kitchen."

The mention of the kitchen reminded Abby that she must call her boss and explain what had happened—he was expecting her for the breakfast shift in the morning and she had no idea how she was going to get there.

"Ethan, I'm sorry, but do you think that we could continue the tour later? I'm meant to be at work at 7:00 tomorrow morning. My car died last month and I need to work out how I'm going to get there on time."

"You've been walking to work? And home I bet, at God knows what hour." He scraped a hand through his hair and didn't even try to cover the frustration and criticism in his voice. "You're lucky that nothing's happened to you. Look, I'll drive you to work in the morning, and we'll try and work out a plan from there. You can borrow a car, of course, but I don't like the idea of you leaving the restaurant on your own late at night, not even by car."

This time Abby wasn't so pleased to have raised a reaction from Ethan. She could see his mind working double time, no doubt trying to work out how he was going to rearrange his morning to accommodate taxiing her around. If he would just accept that she knew how to take care of herself, he wouldn't have to bother.

"Thank you, that's a kind offer," she said, even if it was motivated by his seemingly inexhaustible desire to make decisions for her, "but you've done enough already. I can't ask you to drive me to work. Especially for a breakfast shift."

"You didn't ask," he corrected her, sharply, "but it's what's happening. I'll drive you to work tomorrow and then we'll come up with a plan for the next couple of weeks. Do you still need to call your boss?"

She couldn't believe the nerve of him. True, it was kind of him to offer, but surely one was free to turn down an offer. This wasn't an offer at all, it was an order. He had put her in this impossible situation by insisting that she come to his house, with little idea of where it was and with no means of transport. She had no choice but to agree with him—again. But every time he put her in these impossible situations, she grew more and more frustrated. It's not as if she had no regard for her personal safety. She took reasonable precautions to make sure that she was as safe as possible in her neighborhood; she stuck to the main streets, carried a personal alarm and pepper spray. She had more locks than she could count in her apartment.

If only she had known when she had arrived in the city that these weren't the only safety precautions she should be taking. It wasn't always the obvious threats you had to worry about, she thought to herself.

"No, it's fine," she finally replied. "I'll talk to him in the morning." She could hear the ice returning to her voice. Ethan had the good grace to look a little sheepish.

"I'm sorry if I was a little…terse. It's been a long day." Abby's face softened slightly. He did look exhausted. The last couple of hours couldn't have been easy on him either.

"So, shall we continue the tour upstairs…?" For a second, they both paused. All of a sudden, this situation seemed very personal. Intimate. Up until now, she could have just been a casual visitor. But upstairs? Bedrooms and bathrooms? So far, Abby had tried—and mainly succeeded—to block out the knowledge that she would be sleeping in Ethan Walker's house. She knew that she was obviously not the first guest to get the guided tour, and couldn't help but wonder how many of the tours had included the upstairs as well.

Jealousy…again. Abby recognized the emotion that was making her blood feel hot in her veins. Okay, so she wasn't exactly happy about that. She did not like to think of herself as a jealous woman at the best of times. But jealous about Ethan? That was definitely not good. Abby had no idea how she was going to stop herself being attracted to Ethan if they were living in such close proximity. The kiss that had almost happened earlier had to be the result of adrenaline and being squeezed into a tiny place. It couldn't happen again.

"I thought you'd like these rooms…" Ethan announced as he opened the door to a beautiful living room.

Okay, so maybe they wouldn't be in such close proximity after all. This guest suite was twice the size of Abby's apartment. She gazed around the comfortable looking sitting room, unable to believe that this was all part of her suite. Through an open door she could see the bedroom, complete with the most enormous bed Abby had ever seen, and beyond that, a bathroom, lined with marble and containing a tub the size of a swimming pool. Maybe she wouldn't have to see as much of Ethan as she'd feared. By the looks of it, she could spend weeks and weeks here without ever having to leave her room—or rooms, she corrected herself.

"I'm afraid there's no kitchen up here, but make yourself at home downstairs. Gloria will be in to cook dinner every day so let her know if there's something in particular that you want. Feel free to raid the cupboards and the fridge for breakfast and lunch."

Abby knew that this was the appropriate time to say thank you for everything that Ethan was doing for her—for giving her a safe place to stay and feeding her from his kitchen, but for some reason the words wouldn't come. It seemed as if all of the emotion of the last few hours was finally catching up with her. She managed a couple of steps to the nearest sofa, and slumped down onto the cushions.

Ethan crouched in front of her, as he had in her apartment, clearly concerned that she was about to lose it. He didn't need to worry. That was the last thing she was about to do. Two years of rigid self-protection had taught her better than that. She forced herself to pull her hands back as he reached for them.

She raced through scenarios in her mind, trying to calculate the risk that she had taken in coming here. It was far from an ideal situation. But the shooting in her apartment had forced her hand. She had impressed upon Ethan in the car that she could only stay there if it remained absolutely secret. He'd said that he'd understood, even that he'd speak to the staff, ensure that they kept quiet too, and so for the first time in two years she'd shared the burden of keeping herself safe with another person.

"I'm fine, it's just been a long day. I think I need to turn in." *And get some space from you,* she added to herself. Remembering that he was off-limits was hard enough when they were arguing—Ethan being kind was the last thing she needed.

"If you're sure you're okay…"

"I am." She must have sounded slightly more convincing than she felt, because although Ethan gave her a long look, he wished her goodnight and left.

When he was gone, she dropped her head into her hands. *I am in so much trouble.* Abby groaned and dragged her tired body into the bedroom.

• • •

Ethan was sitting at the kitchen table when Abby appeared at half past five the next morning. She looked cute, he thought. All bed hair and smudged mascara, with the impression of her pillow still on her cheek.

"Morning," she said, her voice cool. "I didn't expect to see you before I left."

"You didn't?" Ethan was surprised; he had told her he was going to drive her. "But I thought that we agreed—"

"I thought you might have asked Thomas to take me."

"Right, and you would have preferred it if I had?" He tried to gauge her mood, sensing that a storm was brewing.

"That's not what I said."

"Well, either way, I'm afraid you're stuck with me this morning.' He smiled cheerily, trying to lift the atmosphere, but it seemed to make her mood worse, rather than better. "Any news on your neighbor?"

"I called the hospital just now. They wouldn't tell me anything other than that she and the baby are stable."

"Well, I guess that's as good as you can hope for after something like that. Will you be ready to leave in half an hour?"

"Of course, just let me have a cup of tea and I'll be ready before you…" She stopped suddenly when she saw his expression. "What is it? Oh God, don't tell me…"

Ethan raised his hands in a gesture of conciliation. "Sorry, no tea."

"No tea?" Abby collapsed into a chair and rested her elbows on the table.

"I can make you a cup of coffee…"

"No, don't bother. God, I hate this bloody country. I think I'm just going to go for a shower, I'll be back down at six."

Ethan watched her retreating back and wondered how he was going to cope with the next few days, or weeks, or however long she was going to be in his house. Even throwing a tantrum about a cup of tea with crazy hair and yesterday's make-up on, she was irresistible. Thank God she had stormed off when she did. If she'd stayed any longer, he would have been forced to kiss her, just to wipe the sulky pout from her lips and try and bring a smile to her face.

He wondered whether him driving her to work would cause her problems. It didn't seem to him that anyone at the diner knew about her former career, or about whatever it was that had made her give it up. Her reaction to his presence at her workplace had shown him that she was keeping pretty big secrets even from those who were closest to her.

He'd do everything he could for now to keep her secret safe. He'd already spoken to his staff to make sure they remembered the confidentiality clauses in their contracts and was pretty sure that there would be no breaches.

He hoped that if he could keep Abby safe, maybe she would listen to him about the film. Sure, he was attracted to her, but it was the film that *needed* her. And any time he felt like he was getting close to her, she threw up the "back off" banners. Getting involved with her personally could put her involvement at risk, and he couldn't—wouldn't—sacrifice this project for the sake of a passing attraction. And if there was one thing that Ethan knew about his attractions to beautiful women, it was that they always passed quickly.

• • •

Abby kicked off her shoes as she walked into Ethan's kitchen. Her feet were screaming and her head was pounding after ten hours of dodging Candy's questions.

When she looked over at the kitchen table it took a moment for it to sink in. When it did, and she finally realized what she was looking at…at that moment she thought that she had never seen anything so beautiful. True, she had thought something very similar about an hour ago when she saw Ethan waiting for her outside the diner, but even Ethan's perfectly chiseled cheekbones and designer stubble had nothing on this.

Stacked on the table were boxes and boxes of tea. And not just any old tea—there was no Californian fruit rubbish here—proper loose-leaf blends that she was pretty sure were only sold by Fortnum and Mason's, as well as good old Twining's, Tetley, PG Tips, Yorkshire, even Ringtons; God only knew where he had been able to find them all.

"Oh my goodness…"

"Did I find the right ones?"

Abby threw him an enormous smile, picking up the boxes one by one. "I can't believe you did this! Where did it all come from? Wait, no, don't tell, I know full well that you would have to deal with the devil himself to get some of these blends and I'd rather not know the details. Just…thank you." She knew she was grinning like an idiot, but she couldn't help it. She seemed to have lost all control of her facial muscles.

"Well, the look on your face this morning…I couldn't risk that happening again. I can't think of anything more terrifying."

"Was I that bad?"

"I'd love to be the perfect gentleman and say, 'No, you were fine,' but let's face it, I'm no gentleman."

I hope not, she thought. *Shit, I really should not be thinking things like that,* she told herself firmly.

"So then, which do we try first?"

"Seriously? You're going to brave proper English tea?" Abby laughed. "Should I have a skinny soy hazelnut extra shot macchiato with foam on hand, just in case you need to rinse the taste out of your mouth?"

Ethan raised an eyebrow at the stereotype. "I think I can risk it without. Do your worst."

"Right then, I need a kettle and a tea pot."

"A kettle and a tea pot?" Ethan pulled a face. "Aren't they the same thing?"

Abby let out a melodramatic sigh. "You have *so* much to learn." Ethan laughed at the look of mock despair on Abby's face. "I need something to heat some water in and something to put the tea and water into once it's boiled."

Ethan retained his poker face while he gestured back towards the table. "Well, why don't you look in the basket and see if there's anything in there you can use."

Abby gave him a suspicious look and glanced at the picnic basket. She hadn't noticed it earlier, hidden behind all the packets of tea. She lifted the lid and laughed. Nestled inside was an electric kettle, a beautiful porcelain tea pot, two delicate cups and saucers, silver teaspoons, and a matching tea strainer.

Abby lifted the teapot out of the hamper and held it up to the light of the window. "Mr. Walker, this may well be the most beautiful thing I have ever seen. I just don't know what to say..."

"It's nothing, I'm just happy to see you happy. I thought you probably deserved something nice after what you've been through in the last twenty-four hours. And I figured anything that might avoid a pout like you had this morning was worth a try. So, my education is in your hands."

Sitting drinking tea with Ethan, Abby had to keep reminding herself of the many very good reasons why she couldn't live this particular fairy tale. This man was not for her. The idea of a knight in shining armor, rescuing her from the grubby diner, just wasn't possible. She'd thrown that away over two years ago, and no amount of wishful thinking would be able to rescue it.

But every time she had herself convinced that anything romantic with Ethan was impossible, doubts started to creep in. Her career was over, but that didn't mean her life was. She'd already been forced into taking a risk by staying here, albeit temporarily. She trusted him. She couldn't say why, but she wouldn't be here if she didn't. So, could she rely on him to keep other secrets too? If being at Ethan's house could stay a secret, then a fling with him could stay secret too…

It could never be anything serious, of course—she'd known that much about Ethan before she even met him. She'd looked back through some magazines after he'd come to the diner, looking for anything she could use to get rid of him. But instead she'd found herself looking at all the women he'd dated. She wasn't short of material. From the dates on the magazines, two weeks of dating Ethan seemed to be pretty average, three was a good run, and four was exceptional. He liked change; a challenge. He wasn't interested in commitment.

"So, Abby, I was thinking," Ethan said, mock-casually. "How would you like to read the script for the movie I was telling you about?" She stared at him, her face dropping as comprehension dawned. "I know you've told me you're not going to change your mind. If you read the script and still don't want to do it, fine. But if there's just a chance that I can persuade you to even think about it … How about it? Just read the script, tell me what you think of it."

His words were like a shot of ice-cold water down the back of Abby's neck. "Ethan, I...I can't." She'd misjudged him. She could only be thankful that he had shown his true colors before any real damage was done. She had been so touched by his thoughtfulness, but now, in light of his request, it was tainted. This was what his gift, his generosity, was really about. He wanted a piece of her. To him, she was just another body that he needed on camera. Well, it wasn't going to work. He clearly hadn't given up on her yet, so the best thing that she could do was just to keep out of his way.

"I'm sorry, Ethan, but I'm exhausted after my shift. I think I'm going to go straight up for a lie down."

"Sure. Is everything okay? I didn't mean to upset you talking about the script. You know that's not what this was about, the tea and everything."

"No, of course." *Yeah, right.* "I'm just tired, I need some time to myself."

"If you're sure..."

"It's fine." Or it would be, as long as she kept her distance.

She didn't think that Ethan *meant* to blackmail her—she was sure that he hadn't made a conscious decision to do so, but this was clearly just how his mind worked. She was just a commodity to be bought and sold, and he would do anything he wanted in order to get his own way.

• • •

She's clearly not *fine*, Ethan thought to himself. He knew it was a risk, bringing up the movie. But he couldn't give up on it. Sitting with her here, comfortable in his kitchen, he was more convinced than ever that she was exactly who he needed. Who the movie needed. But he was stumped about how he was going to persuade her. The tea thing *hadn't* been premeditated; he really had just wanted to do something nice for her after she was so upset this morning. He'd had to do something to get rid of the deep, uncomfortable ache he felt in his chest when worry lines creased her forehead into a frown, when shadows of pain and fear crossed her face. Anything to capture the smile he'd seen come so readily to her lips on-screen, but so rarely in real life.

And it had worked—she'd seemed so much more relaxed with him than she had before, and he'd thought that maybe he was getting somewhere, that staying with him was helping. That it might be worth asking again. Big mistake. The barriers had come straight back up and he was back to square one. It was clear that if he was going to change her mind, gifts weren't the way to do it. He was convinced, however, that if she knew more about the project—the script, the people involved, the quality of the work that had already been completed—then she wouldn't be able to resist. No more trying to talk her into it, he just had to show her that the movie was going to be so good, she couldn't possibly pass it up.

Chapter Five

Keeping her distance from Ethan was proving more difficult than Abby had imagined. The house was enormous, her suite of rooms were beautiful, but day after day she found herself being drawn downstairs. To start with, it seemed reasonable to convince herself that it was the kitchen facilities that were making her move towards that part of the house, but really she knew that she was kidding herself.

She stepped into the kitchen a little before seven-thirty and filled the kettle. She flicked through the paper on the kitchen table as she waited for the water to boil and listened for the sound of Ethan's footsteps in the corridor. For the last three days he had appeared in the kitchen while she was making breakfast, and they had ended up eating together.

It's just a coincidence, she'd told herself the second time it happened. Neither of them had planned it, but they were living together—it made sense that they would bump into each other, especially as she didn't have a kitchen upstairs.

She absolutely, definitely, was not trying to contrive a meeting with Ethan.

So why did she feel so disappointed to be sitting eating her toast alone? It was nothing. She hadn't seen her friends—well, Candy—in days. Even though Ethan had lent her a car—nothing flash, she had insisted—and she could get to work now, she'd decided to take some of her vacation days anyway: a bit of R and R was long overdue.

It was perfectly normal to want a little conversation, and Ethan was the only person around. But deep down she knew that it was more than that. She had been looking forward to seeing him this morning, and the day before...and the day before that. She'd thought that Ethan was feeling the same way. That he was making as much of an effort to spend time with her as she was to spend time with him. But she'd obviously misjudged things. Again. If he had considered this a regular breakfast date, then he'd be here now, or he would at least have let her know that he wouldn't be.

It seemed safer to spend time together in the day. Just because she enjoyed his company didn't mean that she wanted to do something stupid. An evening in Ethan's cozy den would be too intense—she'd proved that to herself two nights ago. Ethan had asked her if she wanted to watch a movie. She'd known that she should say no, stay away from him; but, she had reasoned, sitting in silence together for a couple of hours was unlikely to do any harm.

Half an hour in and it had already felt like the longest evening of her life. She'd thought that an action movie would be a safe choice—no soul-searching, no love scenes. But she hadn't anticipated that the complete lack of intellectual engagement would leave her mind free to wander. And much as she'd tried to stop it, it wandered doggedly in one direction.

Though they had stuck strictly to opposite ends of the sofa, with zero physical contact, every time Ethan shifted his position on the couch, she had wondered whether he was going to move closer. Did he want to? Did she want him to? In the end when the credits rolled she had breathed an enormous sigh of relief and escaped to her room without saying more than a few words. Not an experience she wanted to repeat.

Ever since then she'd avoided Ethan in the evenings. They'd share a quick dinner if he was home from work—she was a guest after all, it would be rude to just eat alone in her room. But as soon as she got the opportunity, she escaped upstairs. Alone.

When the pot of tea was cold and over-brewed, Abby abandoned her vigil at the breakfast table. It was clear that Ethan wasn't going to be showing up any time soon, so she resolved to get on with her day.

When she returned to the house, she found dinner in the oven. She set the table for two and poured the red wine that she knew was Ethan's favorite. If she'd let herself think about it, she would have worried about how much she had missed seeing him this morning, but she was too preoccupied with looking forward to him getting home. It was natural to miss a housemate, she told herself. She had missed having company—that was all. Oh, who was she kidding? She missed him. There was no getting away from it. Five days of living together and her resolve was all but gone. And until he had missed their breakfast date that morning, Abby had suspected that Ethan felt the same way.

She glanced at the clock on the microwave again, incredulous that only three more minutes had passed. Three more minutes of sitting at a set dinner table, trying not to polish off her wine. Three more minutes of wondering where Ethan had got to. She tried again to remember whether Ethan had said anything yesterday about being out all day, and most of the evening. He couldn't have done. She would have remembered—it wasn't like she hadn't had the opportunity to think about it. And anyway, if he'd known that he wasn't going to be home, he wouldn't have asked Gloria to leave dinner in the oven. No, something had come up, and he'd decided not to come home. Clearly, he'd received a better offer.

At nine o'clock she blew out the candles, turned off the music, fetched her book from her bedroom, and moved to the sofa.

At 10:00 she started un-setting the table; returning cutlery to the drawer, glasses to the cupboard. Removing any trace of the disastrous evening.

And at eleven, she walked up the stairs, hesitating as she turned out the kitchen light, thinking how big a fool she might have made of herself had Ethan come home and found her haunting the kitchen Miss Havisham style.

Whatever it was that she'd thought was happening between them, she'd obviously imagined it. He was charming her, not because he wanted her, but because he needed her for his film. If he was with someone else tonight, then that was clearly the answer. She was just another actress to him.

• • •

The next morning, Abby stayed in her room until she heard the gates open and Ethan's car pulling out of the driveway. At least that meant that he had come home sometime last night. Or maybe this morning. She knew it was childish to hide, but she just couldn't face him. It didn't matter that Ethan didn't know that she'd sat at the table, waiting for him, for hours. She knew, and she knew what it meant. What she had felt. She couldn't look Ethan in the eye this morning; she couldn't risk him seeing all of that written on her face.

By the time evening came round, she felt like she had spent the day in a daze. If she had been asked for an account of her time, she doubted that she could remember more than an hour. The whole day had felt like a held breath, waiting for Ethan to come home, and she still hadn't decided how she was going to play it. She was tempted to stay in her room again. But that would mean two whole days of not seeing Ethan. She couldn't stand not knowing where he was last night—and she couldn't bear to ask him.

She walked to the window when she heard the car in the driveway, hoping the shutters would hide her spying. He was home. Abby ran through her options quickly. Be casually waiting for him downstairs. Be out for the evening—maybe a little late to be thinking about now—or hide. Hiding it was.

Hiding from him wasn't a bad plan, it was just harder to accomplish when she was in his home. Did he know she was home? The knock on her door suggested that he did.

"Abby, you in there?"

Abby hesitated, but knew that letting him in was inevitable. She'd crack sooner or later, and she supposed sooner might make her seem a little saner.

She opened the door a crack. Ethan was leaning against the wall opposite her door, patiently waiting for her to do what he expected.

"Hi."

"Hello." She knew she sounded frosty, but she couldn't help it. He didn't even know that he'd stood her up, but that didn't mean she couldn't be cross with him—right?

"Are you hungry?"

"No." The denial was out of her mouth before she had a chance to think about it.

"Have you eaten already?"

"No." Her voice was smaller this time.

"So, do you want to come down, have some dinner?"

She looked him in the eye. She smiled. She couldn't help it.

"Yes."

• • •

"So, good day at the office?" She tried to keep her voice level, make small talk, but the comfortable atmosphere that had developed between them over the past few days had disappeared.

"Oh, the usual, you know, meetings for most of the day, trying to wade through contracts for the rest of it. I'm sorry I didn't see you yesterday. I missed you."

Where did that come from? Abby met his eyes, which were smiling at her across the table.

"Last night..." she started, not knowing how to ask without sounding like a bunny boiler.

"Last night I was battling through a mountain of paperwork. I didn't leave the office until after three, and I had a meeting back there at eight. I wanted to clear my desk as much as I could because I'm going to be working from home for the rest of the week, and maybe next week too. It didn't seem right, inviting you here and then abandoning you all day. I hope that's okay…"

For the first time that day she felt a smile forming on her lips, and finally recognized what should have been obvious from the first time she'd seen Ethan, down that stinking alley beside the diner. Her falling for him was inevitable. She was never going to be able to fight this attraction, the need to be near him. "It's okay. It's better than okay. I'm not sure what I'm going to do with myself while you're working, though. I'm not used to sitting around with nothing to do."

"Well I'm sure I can think of something."

Abby raised an eyebrow and laughed.

"Not like that." Ethan laughed back. "Unless that *is* what you meant, of course…"

Abby shook her head, but still smiled. Okay, so this was new. There had been some subtle flirting between them over the past couple of days, a glance held too long, the brush of a hand on a glass, squeezing a little too close to get through a doorway. But this felt different—more exciting, more dangerous, more deliberate. Maybe Ethan had thought of her as often today as she had thought of him.

"I meant that I've a stack of scripts to read," Ethan continued. "Maybe you could take a look and let me know what you think?"

She froze. Was this another trick, another tactic? Ethan clearly read what she was thinking because he hurriedly explained.

"Not *that* script. Unless you want to, of course, but that's not what I meant. I get sent so many, and there are only so many that my assistant and I can get through. If you wanted something to do you're welcome to read them—let me know if you think any of them are good."

Abby weighed it up—he might slip *the* script into the pile without her realizing it. But whatever bad decisions she may be about to make about her personal life, she still knew where she stood professionally. Reading the script wouldn't change anything; however much she loved it. She sensed that something had changed for them both today; the time apart, the longest they had spent since they met, had helped her realize how much she wanted him. No one even knew she was here; anything that happened between them could stay just as secret.

"Sure, why not."

• • •

"So, there's something I need to talk to you about—I'm having a guest over for dinner on Friday and I thought you might want to make yourself scarce…"

Abby's stomach plummeted. How could she have read things so badly? They had just spent a lovely couple of hours enjoying dinner, chatting, catching up. She'd thought something had changed between them. But she'd got it completely wrong. He was just being friendly, working from home. It didn't mean anything. He had invited someone for dinner and he wanted her out of the way. Well it couldn't be more obvious what this was about, could it. He had invited her to stay as a houseguest, but now he had a date and he wanted her out of the way. She'd obviously misread all of the signals, thinking they were getting closer, when all the time he was seeing someone else.

"Oh, yes, of course. I won't be in the way. I can stay at Candy's if you like, so you can have the whole place to yourselves." The last thing she wanted was to witness Ethan trying to seduce another woman.

"Abby..."

"No, it's fine. I understand."

"Abby, I really don't think you do. I'd like nothing more than for you to join us."

Oh, I bet you would.

"There goes that dirty mind of yours."

She kicked herself. Ethan could read her like a book.

"I'm not talking about a date, Abby. It's a business dinner, with the director of the movie. We've a lot to talk about and he suggested doing it over dinner. Here. He practically invited himself actually. I just wanted to warn you because I didn't think you'd want to bump into him on the stairs."

"Oh." *Oh indeed.*

"But I take it you won't be joining us?"

"I...no. But thank you for warning me."

"You thought I had a date? That I was bringing her here?"

There was no point denying it, she knew that he had seen exactly what she was thinking. "Yes."

"If you think that then I don't think you really understand me at all. I don't know how you could think that I would be interested in another woman when I have you here." He reached out and covered Abby's hand with his own.

Abby didn't dare breathe, let alone move. This was crunch time. No going back.

Chapter Six

Abby looked up slowly and her eyes met Ethan's. His hold on her hand tightened and he pulled her out of her seat and onto his lap. She stopped with her face a few inches from his. She couldn't believe that this was happening. That she was letting this happen. When she had arrived at his house, she had been so sure that being involved with Ethan would be a disaster. But now she couldn't think of a single reason not to do this. Okay, there were lots of reasons not to do this, but none of them seemed to matter at this precise moment. She wouldn't have to tell him anything. No one else need ever know about them. And there might be a million reasons against doing what she wanted, but there was one *very* compelling reason *to* do it. She wanted him; she *really* wanted him.

And that in itself felt like a little miracle. As she felt the electricity from where their hands touched spark through her body, she let out a little gasp. She had thought that this was gone for good, this need to be close to someone, to want to touch them, to be touched. She closed her eyes and waited to feel Ethan's lips on hers. And waited. And waited. She opened her eyes to find that he had hesitated with just millimeters of air separating their lips. He was making sure that she was sure, that this was her choice.

Oh, she was sure alright. She sighed and leant forwards, finally closing the distance between them. She'd spent days wondering about how his hair would feel beneath her hands, and she couldn't help but indulge herself and gently grab a handful of it to pull him closer. It was clear from his reaction that, until that moment, Ethan had been holding back. As she tugged gently he let out a sound not far from a growl and bit at her lower lip. She smiled against his mouth. She felt Ethan's hand move to mirror her own, cupping the back of her neck beneath her hair, holding her tight. His other arm curled tight around her waist.

He deepened the kiss and she moaned as his tongue explored her mouth. Her hands pressed against his chest, but this time with no thoughts of pushing him away. Instead they dropped down, tracing the lines of his abs, feeling each defined muscle, and slipped between the buttons of his shirt. They were acting of their own accord when they started unbuttoning it. She wasn't thinking at all, she just knew that she wanted, needed, it gone. She fumbled, desperate to get to skin, and finally pushed the sides of his shirt apart to claim her prize. But as she leaned forward to press her lips to his chest, she felt his hands, warm, strong, and insistent, reach for the bottom of her T-shirt and start to lift. They pulled her tee up sharply, and Ethan moved back, pulled the shirt over her head.

In the fraction of the second his lips were away from hers, the Ethan-fog that had filled Abby's brain lifted, and she panicked, clutching the T-shirt back to her chest, desperately trying to cover herself. It was a reflex, nothing more, she told herself as she tried to slow her breathing and loosen her grip. No one had removed her clothes since the day of the fake audition. She'd not been undressed in front of anyone, other than medical professionals, since then. She knew that Ethan wouldn't hurt her. Knew that he was undressing her for no reason other than he liked her, desired her, wanted her.

But the cold shot of fear she'd felt in her belly had stopped her dead.

And now that she had the space to think about it, this was getting rather out of hand. A kiss was one thing, but this was all going way too fast. And she had no one to blame but herself.

Unperturbed, and with his usual self-confident grin, Ethan leaned back in his chair and pulled Abby with him.

"Sorry about that, I guess I was getting a little carried away," Ethan said, as Abby turned her body away from him and pulled her T-shirt back on.

"Don't apologize; I think you'll find I was the one who started it. I don't even remember undoing your shirt, but..." She traipsed a finger across his chest, tracing the line of a perfectly defined pectoral.

"You're not hearing any complaints from me..."

"And it's not that I don't want to...it's just things were going so fast..."

He silenced her with a sweet kiss on the lips. "Stop apologizing. Whatever you want to do is fine with me. Just make sure that the second you change your mind, you let me know."

Abby laughed and nestled closer into Ethan's shoulder. "I promise you'll be the first person I call. But right now I think I should go to bed—alone—before I get any more carried away. I'm fairly sure I can't be trusted around you."

"How about I see you to your door?"

"I'd like that."

Abby could feel Ethan's eyes on her arse as she climbed the steep stairs from the staff part of the house. The yoga pants had seemed like the perfect choice for an evening of hiding in her room, but now, with Ethan's eyes perfectly level with the skin-tight Lycra, she started to question her choice. All doubts fled, however, when she felt Ethan's hand sculpting the curve of her bum. She looked back over her shoulder and gave him a mock scowl. He laughed and gave her a light slap before pushing her on up the rest of the steps.

"These stairs are severely testing my patience," Ethan said gruffly.

The tension that had been dissipated by their kiss returned as they approached Abby's rooms. They both stopped outside her door and Abby closed her eyes and raised her face for a goodnight kiss. She wasn't expecting the intensity of the kiss when it came. Ethan pressed her against the door and his hands on her hips lifted her closer, molding her body into his. Abby was left in no doubt about the strength of Ethan's desire for her and she groaned as she pressed herself against his erection.

Abby pulled herself away and rested her head back against the door.

"Nice try," she said, gasping for breath, knowing that she had been only moments away from changing her mind, opening the door, and dragging Ethan in with her.

"Can't blame a guy for trying."

"I'd have been upset if you hadn't. But goodnight." She kissed Ethan on the lips, a long, lingering kiss, infinitely sweeter than before.

She couldn't rush this.

Her control on this situation was slipping away, and part of her wanted to loosen her grip and just let it all happen. It was impossible to think straight when Ethan was kissing her. Or had just kissed her. Or was about to kiss her. But the shiver of fear she'd felt when Ethan had removed her T-shirt reminded her of what had happened last time she wasn't on her guard. She needed to know that the risk involved in this situation could be managed. That she wasn't just falling into it because she didn't know how not to.

There were other things to come to terms with too. She knew that Ethan would walk away eventually—his short attention span where women were concerned was no secret, and was only the reason she could consider letting anything happen between them at all. But that didn't mean it would be easy when the time came.

• • •

Ethan sat at the kitchen table, waiting for Abby to appear. It was nearly eight—she was always up by now. Perhaps she was regretting their kiss and was too embarrassed to face him. Not that they could get up to much even if she were here. Gloria had turned up at seven, and was happily pottering away in the kitchen, cleaning through the cupboards and making a start on lunch.

He wondered if Abby had slept as badly as he had. After a kiss like that, and knowing that she was under the same roof, he'd tossed and turned for hours before eventually dropping off. Even with a few hours' sleep behind him, he didn't feel particularly rested.

Eventually, Abby appeared. He saw the deep breath she took as she walked into the room, and the way she set her shoulders, and suspected that she had been building up to this for a while. He also saw the way her shoulders sagged as she spotted Gloria, and couldn't help a smug grin. She was obviously hoping they could be alone together this morning.

She went to pour herself a cup of tea from the pot that he'd made for her and glanced back at where he was sitting. He threw a tiny wink her way, hoping that she knew that he had *not* planned to start this morning with company. She quickly looked back at her tea, her face glowing.

Gloria talked on and on, asking Ethan and Abby about their plans for the day. Ethan didn't think that they had done anything to give themselves away, not that he minded too much, but he knew that Abby would be uncomfortable if anyone knew what had happened last night. They certainly hadn't *said* anything that might, but from the looks Gloria kept throwing, first at Abby, then at Ethan, he knew that she suspected something was going on. Fortunately, she kept whatever she was thinking to herself, but he could see that they were going to have to be careful around her if they wanted to keep their secret.

The time dragged by slowly as he waited for Gloria to leave. Every time he thought she was about to go she seemed to find another cupboard that needed cleaning, some prep to do for their meal that evening. A sudden and overwhelming desire to bake cookies. Eventually he realized that he wasn't going to get Abby on her own, mumbled something about needing to start work, and disappeared in the direction of the study.

He'd left his mug of coffee, fresh from the pot, on the counter, hoping that Abby would take the hint and bring it to him. He listened to her footsteps getting closer, but just before she reached the door his cell phone started to ring. He checked the display. Shit. He really had to get this. He answered the phone while walking to the door—just because he had to work didn't mean he planned on letting Abby get away. Her footsteps had stopped outside the door, and he suspected that unless he intervened, she was about to lose her nerve.

He opened the door and hooked a finger into the belt loop of her jeans, pulling her inside. He didn't let go until she had placed both cups of coffee safely on his desk, and then he pulled until she fell into his lap. He continued talking the whole time, his conversation never faltering. Abby tried to stand, maybe thinking that she was in his way, but he tightened his arm around her waist.

When Ethan finally ended the call, Abby opened her mouth to speak. Before she could get a word out, Ethan bent down and kissed her gently, not wanting to rush her, knowing that it was his impatience last night that had cut things short. But just as he was thinking about how good it was to have her back in his arms, his phone started to ring again and he couldn't not reach for it—it could be important. He pulled away.

"I'm sorry, I really should get this."

She kissed him gently on the lips and wriggled out of the arm that had now loosened from around her waist. "It's fine. Work now, play later."

Ethan groaned and hit answer.

• • •

Play later. As Ethan hung up—another call from a financier, worried about the status of the movie—those were two words that stuck in his mind. Being distracted from work by just thinking about a kiss was not part of his plan. He wanted Abby; wanted to be able throw over his whole day's work and spend it with her, but that's not who he was. He couldn't afford to slip up now, not with everything so uncertain with the movie. If Abby would just agree ... Did their new intimacy make that more likely or less? It had been a huge risk to kiss her, he knew that now. But at the time, he hadn't thought it through. She'd looked so beautiful, he'd just done it. But then resisting hadn't exactly been working either.

Perhaps if they were closer, personally, she'd open up to him. Explain why she thought she couldn't take the part, and then once he knew, he could deal with it. It wasn't the *only* reason of course.

He had his choice of women. He left every party with a pocket full of phone numbers that women had subtly slipped there. Of course most of them were just interested in what he could do for their careers. He'd dated a few women over the years. Okay, maybe "a few" was a bit of an understatement, but he'd never felt so consumed by someone before, much less someone he'd only kissed a couple of times. He'd never put aside work commitments for a woman. Before Abby he hadn't supposed that such a thing was possible.

It was because she was important to the movie, he reasoned to himself. That's why he couldn't get her off his mind. That's why it felt so important to explore this...this thing between them. But here he was rescheduling meetings so that he could be in the same room as her. They weren't even talking, but it made him happy just to know that she was sitting near him.

He wondered about the script in the middle of the pile. She knew him pretty well by now. Understood his tactics. Would she be expecting it? He felt uneasy anyway. Should he change his mind? Tell her? But it wasn't like it would force her to say yes to him. It would just mean that she would be making a more informed decision. She would be perfectly at liberty to say no if that was what she really wanted.

"You've been staring into space for the last five minutes. How is working from home going?" Abby's voice broke into his thoughts.

He spun his chair so that he was facing her. "You know it's impossible for me to work this morning, and you know it's your fault."

"What, me?" She smiled as he came over to where she had settled in for the morning, and then squealed as he threw the script she was reading on the floor, sat down on the couch, and pulled her on top of him. "You do know that it's only four minutes to eleven." Eleven was the time they'd agreed on for a "coffee" break. "I should make you wait, you know, if I give an inch now…"

"You give me the extra four minutes and I promise I'll make it worth your while."

Abby's answer was lost in a passionate kiss.

Suddenly, Ethan broke away. "There's something I have to tell you."

Breathless, Abby seemed to consider this. "I'm not sure anything good has ever followed that statement."

"I'm sorry, but I hid the script in that pile."

He could see from the look on her face that she had understood him, and that it wasn't a surprise to her, and she wasn't angry. She had been expecting him to try and trick her, but she had taken the risk anyway. Was this her softening to the idea of making the movie? Or did she think that reading the script wouldn't change her mind? Either way, he knew he couldn't pressure her. He wanted her to change her mind—of course he did. But pressure wasn't going to get him what he wanted.

He didn't want to think about the implications of what he'd just done. When it came down to it, he'd put protecting Abby's feelings ahead of doing what was best for his movie. Between that, and how distracted he'd been over the past few days, she was not currently good for his career. But the ends *would* justify the means. When she finally agreed to do the movie, it wouldn't matter that he'd spent a couple of weeks with his mind not exactly on the job.

• • •

"The script? In here?" She knew she sounded like a simpleton, but she had to be certain what he was saying. He'd tricked her, but then he'd told her. Should she forgive him just because he'd had an attack of conscience? But then it's not like she hadn't expected it. She knew Ethan well enough to know that he hadn't given up on her. She sighed. She couldn't think through all the implications of this sitting here. She'd barely been out of the house in days and all of a sudden the cabin fever started to burn away at her.

"I think I need to go for a walk…"

She saw the apprehension on Ethan's face. No wonder. He'd blown his own plan out of the water.

"Want some company?"

She would think clearer without him, but still, the idea of walking in the hills with Ethan was hard to resist. Maybe if she could see him outside of the house, outside of danger-filled situations or domestic intimacy, if they could just talk like normal people, she could get a handle on how it was she actually felt about him.

"Okay. Only…"

"Only you don't want us to be seen together?"

"Right." She wished she could offer an explanation for this. She knew she sounded like a crazy person. But she couldn't tell him why she was so insistent on secrecy, couldn't tell him what had happened to her. Telling Ethan, peeling back the layers of her self-protection and showing the most painful parts of her past … She couldn't expose herself like that. It was what her attackers wanted—to shame her, humiliate her. It would be as if she'd never left that room, as if the camera had never switched off.

And to tell Ethan the whole truth, she'd have to trust that he would do what *she* thought was best. To follow *her* plan for dealing with the situation. And as much as she believed that Ethan wouldn't intentionally do anything to hurt her, she couldn't rule out him charging in and doing something stupid, believing it was for the best thing.

"Don't worry, it's fine. I know your terms." He made her sound so cold. "I know a trail. It's really hidden away—we won't see anyone."

"Meet you by the door in five?"

She dug her trainers out of her holdall and sat on the bed to pull on socks and shoes. It seemed strange to be doing something so normal with Ethan. It still struck her as strange at the oddest moments that her current housemate, host, lover? whatever—*Ethan*—was Ethan bloody Walker.

He was waiting for her when she got to the bottom of the stairs, and as she reached him he produced a baseball cap from behind his back. He pulled it firmly onto her head before taking her sunglasses from her hand and placing them on her nose, stroking behind her ear slightly as he eased the arms through her hair.

"There, the perfect disguise."

She smiled at him. He was teasing a little, but she was sure that he was doing this to make her feel more comfortable. She stretched up and planted a soft kiss on Ethan's lips.

"Thank you."

• • •

After half an hour of walking, Abby finally felt like her head was clearing. There was nothing like fresh air and exercise to make her feel more in control of her life. And being out here had helped her come to an important decision. It was time for her to leave Ethan's and go back home to her drug- and violence-filled neighborhood. After last night, that seemed like the less complicated option. She'd spoken to the hospital this morning and her neighbor was out of danger; she'd had the baby, and both were doing well. She'd spoken to the police as well, and they'd told her it was a random attack, and there was no danger in going back.

She had made up her mind, and now there was only one hurdle. She looked up at Ethan and wondered how he was going to take this. She was probably worrying over nothing, she told herself. He might even be glad to get rid of her. But if that was the case, why would he have arranged to work from home? No, it was wishful thinking. Ethan would want her where he knew she was safe, and where he could drop not-so-subtle hints about taking the role in his movie. Whichever way she approached it, this wasn't going to be easy. *Might as well dive right in...*

"So, I'm going to go back home tomorrow."

Ethan's head whipped round as he stopped walking. "Don't be ridiculous. Of course you're not."

Abby placed her hands on her hips in indignation. It seemed that the recent developments in their relationship had done nothing to soften Ethan's controlling side. On the contrary, she feared she had made things much worse on that front.

"Ethan, I can't stay here. Not like this. You want me to make this movie. I get that. I also get that you'll never stop trying to persuade me to do it. You tried to trick me, and I can't live with someone who's constantly trying to catch me out. Surely you can see it's impossible for me to stay." Even though she had been expecting him to try and convince her, it still stung to know that she had been right.

"I've said I'm sorry. It was a mean trick, but I really do think that if you just thought about it for a while, you might change your mind—"

"Ethan, stop!"

This had to end now. They couldn't carry on like this. She couldn't even speak another word to him, let alone do anything else, unless he agreed to stop asking, once and for all. She had to make him see why it was impossible for her to make the film, otherwise he was going to carry on relentlessly.

"Ethan, you don't seem to be listening to me. It's not that I won't make your movie. I can't." Choosing every word with infinite care, she tried to tell him enough of her story to make him understand that she could never go back. And she could never be completely honest with him. "When I first came to LA, something happened…and if I were to be in the limelight…there are people who … I could get hurt." She hardened her gaze as she looked him in the eye. "I am not prepared to risk that, however good your movie is. So please stop asking. If *this*, whatever this is, is just about trying to convince me to change my mind…"

Ethan pulled her to his chest and held her tight, one hand tangling in her hair. "It's not. I promise. But I want you to tell me who hurt you. Who might hurt you. And I swear that I will make it go away."

She looked up, desperate to believe him. "I can't tell you," she said, and dropped her gaze, hiding the tears gathering in her eyes. "There's nothing you can do. You getting involved would only make things worse. I should still go home," she insisted.

"Stay," Ethan said, threading his fingers through the hair, cupping her nape, holding her protectively against his chest. "Stay and I promise I won't mention you taking the part. I won't ask any more questions. The first time I do, I'll help you pack myself. I promise you're safe here."

One last chance, she told herself. But the minute he mentioned it, she would be out the door.

Chapter Seven

Lunch had seemed like an interminable episode of lingering glances and pregnant pauses. It had taken superhuman levels of restraint to stay on the opposite side of the table and not to try and persuade her to swap food for sex. But she had been right about not wanting to rush into anything. He knew for a fact that she was hiding something big from him and she didn't trust him enough yet to tell him.

Lunch over, they had headed back to the study, holding hands like a couple of teenagers. They'd been working in silence for over an hour now. Ethan was just starting to wonder whether she was okay when he heard a sniff from the armchair behind him. He looked around and saw Abby hastily wipe a tear from her cheek. It looked as if she was reading the script. *The* script. He'd offered to take it back, but she'd said no. That she'd like to read it, even though it could never change her mind. So what to do now? Interrupt? Leave her to it?

She must have felt his eyes on her because she looked up and met his eyes across the room. She gave a small smile and went back to her reading. Ethan walked to the bookshelf on the other side of the room, took down a box of tissues, and walked over to Abby's chair. He placed the tissues on the arm of the chair, leaned down and planted a gentle kiss on her forehead, then returned to his desk. A sneaky glance at the papers on her lap confirmed his suspicions. She was reading it.

Would reading the script change her mind? She swore that it wouldn't, but perhaps it still could, perhaps she would feel the same about the script as he did. But if she took the part—and saved his career in the process—what would it cost her? He could see how frightened she was. He only wished that she trusted enough to confide in him. To let him help her, as he was certain that he could. And she was capable of changing her mind—at first she'd been determined to have nothing to do with him, and look where they were now. Maybe she'd change her mind about the movie too. She needed time to read the script, to consider it, so he decided to leave her for now—they could discuss it over dinner. The idea of hearing what she thought of it made him unexpectedly nervous. It wasn't just because he wanted her to take the part. It was more than that. It mattered that she thought that it was good for its own sake. That it was a worthwhile project. That it would make as big an impression on her as it had on him. Suddenly he realized that her opinion would mean more to him than anyone else's.

"I need to make a call. I'll go into the kitchen and leave you in peace."

• • •

She watched him walk out of the study and got back to her reading. By the end of the first page she had known that this must be the script he was talking about. It was beautiful, breath-taking. She couldn't believe that he wanted her to play the lead. She would love to do it. It was the sort of role she had always dreamed about. Vulnerable but steely, it would have been a fabulous showcase for her. She wondered who would play it now. There were a number of actresses she thought might be able to pull it off, but Ethan obviously thought she was the right one. She wished she could do it. She had never wished so much that things were different. That she had been more careful.

It was painfully bittersweet reading the script. She wasn't normally immodest, but she knew that she would have been good in the role. All through drama school and her apprenticeship on the soap opera, this was the sort of role that she'd dreamed of.

Now she had found it. But reading the script didn't feel how she'd thought it would. Ethan had been so certain that it would change her mind, but of course it hadn't. It had just made the dull ache she always felt when she thought of her lost career, her lost dreams, into a sharp stab in her breast.

She read through the last page, put the script down, and wiped the tears from her eyes as she went to find Ethan. He had been gone for a couple of hours and she missed him already. This was not a good sign for what she might feel like when all this was over. She was under no illusions that what they had was going to be anything lasting. Even if it weren't for her past, Ethan's would have been enough to convince her that she couldn't get too involved. She knew that soon enough he would tire of her as he had of every other woman in his life. She would have to deal with missing him then, but right now she could walk to the kitchen and be in the circle of his arms in under a minute. Worrying about the future would save for later.

"You read it," he murmured into her hair, kissing the top of her head. It wasn't a question.

"I did." She lifted her cheek away from him chest and looked up at him.

"And?"

"I loved it. You knew I would."

"You think it's good?"

"I do. I think it's brilliant. Beautiful. I wish…"

He smiled at her, and she knew that he was jumping to conclusions.

"So, do you think—"

"Ethan." She looked away again, and buried her face in his chest. "I loved the script. I wish more than anything that I could make the movie. I wish it were a case of being able to do what I wanted. But I'm afraid it doesn't change anything. I've told you before. It's not that I won't do it. I can't."

"Abby, come on," he said, leaning back and tilting up her chin with a gentle finger. "Please tell me what's wrong. What happened. I'm sure that there's nothing so bad that between us we can't see a way past it. Forget the movie. I want to help you; won't you at least trust me enough to tell me what the problem is?"

For a fraction of a second, she thought about it. Thought about what it might feel like to share the burden of this secret, the threat that hung over her every day. And then she thought about having to explain it all to him. Relive her fear and disgust as the words passed her lips and hazy images flashed through her mind.

And who was to say he'd even believe her? No one believed the others it had happened to. It was just assumed that they were fame hungry, ambitious, at the very least overwhelmingly naïve. She couldn't bear to see that judgment on Ethan's face.

"I can't tell you."

She heard him take a long, deep breath. Felt tension in his arms, his chest, his shoulders, as he pulled her close again. Eventually, he spoke. "Okay."

"Okay?"

"Okay. We don't have to talk about it now."

Abby smiled weakly into his chest. He hadn't given up; she was sure that that was too much to hope for. But until now it had been difficult to tease out whether he liked her as an actress, or for who she really was. But right now, letting her win the battle for a change, she felt like it was really *her* that he wanted.

"Would you do one thing for me?" Maybe she had spoken, or thought, too soon.

Abby looked up at him with a wry grin. "I don't think I should say yes until I know what it is..."

He raised an eyebrow in return. "Nothing like that...well, not today anyway..." He held her gaze and she could feel her whole body growing warm. "I was wondering if you would read for me. I understand that you think that you can't do the movie, but maybe you could read a scene. Just for me?"

Abby drew in a breath. She wanted to. So much. What harm could it do if it was just the two of them here? She knew him too well not to know that he hoped that this might be the thing to change her mind. But she didn't really care. She wished so much that she could make this movie. If things were different it could have launched her career. It still could, she supposed, but at too high a price. If the photos came out, everything would change. That was the power that her abusers held over her. It wasn't enough that they assaulted and humiliated her once; if they wanted to, if they thought they'd make a buck or two, they could sell the photos and invite every person in western world to witness her degradation.

Her parents would be intolerable—a thin veneer of support, backed up by a massive dose of "I told you so" and never being welcome at a family function ever again. And once the tabloids got hold of them, her life would be unbearable.

But she could read for him now. She missed it. Acting was what she loved, what she had always loved. Not saying the words, hitting her marks, but *becoming* another person. Speaking their words and thinking their thoughts and feeling what they felt. Completely occupying another life. Maybe if she read for Ethan, she could feel a little of the old rush again. Just this once.

"Okay."

It was Ethan's turn to be surprised. "Really?!"

"I'll read for you, if you like. You do realize the pressure has been piled on rather high though. I'm bound not to live up to expectations."

Ethan picked her up and spun her round, planting a firm kiss on her lips. She let out a squeal and Ethan brought her gently back to the ground without loosening the arms around her. "I can't believe you said yes. Thank you," he murmured, his forehead resting on hers.

"Don't thank me yet," she whispered back, not wanting to break the connection between them, but unsure of how to handle the growing tension. She was suddenly worried that she would disappoint him. And if she wasn't the actress she thought he was, would the chemistry between them be lost? Would he want her at all? "Have you ever considered in all this that I might be terrible? Maybe I'll read and you'll be relieved that I won't do the movie anyway. You'll be begging me to stop after the first line."

"I know you'll be incredible."

"And if I'm not? If you're disappointed? If you don't want me anymore?"

Ethan smiled down at her. "There's nothing in the world that could make me not want you."

How she wished that were true. But he did want her now. That would have to be enough. Abby smiled against his lips. She hoped she lived up to his expectations, but there were enough real obstacles between them right now. She didn't have to go making up new ones.

"So, dinner first or reading first?"

"I think I need more time before I read. Do you mind? I'll need to read the whole script again before I can even think about one scene."

"Ever the professional. I'm impressed."

"Like I said, don't be yet. I'm not sure I can handle the pressure as it is."

"No pressure." He dropped another kiss on the top of her head. "Whenever you feel ready."

"Ethan…" She had to be sure he understood, just because she was saying yes to this didn't mean—

"I know."

• • •

Abby read through the scene one last time. She hadn't asked him what he would like her to read. She knew which scene it had to be. The heroine of the movie lays her heart on the line. Tells her lover how she feels for him, and gets knocked back. Abby could feel her pain, her heartbreak, radiating from the page. She tried to take it into every cell so that her whole body was consumed by this woman's love, and her pain.

After dinner Abby had had her doubts. Everything was good between her and Ethan right now. Better than good. What if this ruined everything? What if she was terrible and he didn't want her anymore? What if she was good, really good, and he started to put pressure on her again? She'd have to move out. Put distance between them. That was the last thing she wanted. Well, it was now or never. She would never have a chance to read for a Hollywood producer again. Might as well take her kicks where she could get them.

She found Ethan in the den flicking through cable channels without paying them any attention.

"I'm ready." She watched the smile spread over his face, all of his features consumed by it, and she felt her knees weaken slightly. He could be so…distracting, without even trying. "Do you want to go back to the study?"

"No, let's stay in here," Ethan replied, walking towards her, then maneuvering her over in front of the couch. He pulled an armchair opposite so he could watch her in comfort. Abby shifted her weight from foot to foot. When she had agreed, she knew that this wouldn't exactly be a breeze. But she hadn't expected this. These weren't her usual professional nerves. She had noticed those developing earlier without concern. Professional nerves were good. She used them to sharpen her performance. To stop herself getting lazy or failing to prepare. No, these nerves were entirely personal. If tonight went wrong, she was sure that Ethan would feel differently about her. She could be about to tumble from her pedestal and crash unceremoniously to the ground.

• • •

When she finished, she looked up at Ethan. His face was impossible to read. Oh God. He hadn't liked it. She hadn't felt so vulnerable since…since…

"Wha—"

She didn't get a chance to finish her question. Ethan strode over to her and took her face in his hands. Until he wiped them away with his thumbs, she hadn't noticed the tears streaming down her cheeks. They weren't stopping. He hadn't liked it, and now she was going to break down in front of him. She tried desperately to pull herself together. To rein in the tears at least a little bit. She couldn't remember the last time she'd cried like this. She'd certainly never cried like this in front of anyone else. During her performance she'd tapped into her darkest moments, her greatest fears, her sharpest grief to bring the scene to life, and now she couldn't find the off button. The emotions coursed through her like a flood.

"Hey, hey, don't cry." Ethan gathered her to his chest and stroked her hair. "Shhh," he soothed, kissing the top of her head and pulling her down to sit next to him on the couch. Abby sniffled into his shirt, the tears starting to slow.

"Abby, that was…I just don't know what to say. You were amazing. Except amazing isn't a big enough word. You were incredible. Truly. Please don't be upset."

He liked it. Abby breathed a sigh of relief. She had been so sure for just a second that he had hated it. That she was going to lose everything around her. Again.

"I'm sorry." She tried to sit up but Ethan's arms around her wouldn't budge. Her words were muffled as she spoke into his chest. "I think I might have stayed in character a little too long. The tears sort of took me by surprise." Apparently convinced she wasn't going to break down on him again, Ethan loosened his hold. Abby sat up and met his eyes. "Was it really okay?"

"Abby, you were incredible. I don't know what to say."

Abby smiled. Not the disaster that she feared then. Apart from the howling. But from the way that his hand, which had been stroking her shoulder, was subtly making its way to her breast, she hadn't scared him off yet.

Meeting his eyes, she saw a new intensity there. Before she had a chance to register what it might mean, his lips were on hers. She closed her eyes, yielding to the irresistible sensations of Ethan's lips on hers, and opened her mouth, encouraging him to give more.

Her hands reached for his shirt: she wanted, *needed*, to feel his skin beneath her hands again, to finish what they'd started the night before. Images of that bare chest, his hard muscles and fierce gaze had haunted her all night. Running her fingertips over the shifting muscles in his back, she moaned and then slid her hands around to his chest. She traced the lines of his muscles, exploring, teasing, and slowly unbuttoned his shirt.

As Ethan moved away to pull the sleeves off his arms, Abby lay back on the couch and drank in the sight of him. Without feeling even a trace of vulnerability, or a second of doubt, she let her gaze roam over tanned pecs, a scattering of hair on his chest, a tempting trail down below his waistband. Her fingers ached to reach for his buckle, to explore further, but Ethan's hands stopped her.

"I'm feeling underdressed, I think it's only fair that you go next." His voice was gentle, a little breathless, and she sensed his restraint after their false start yesterday. Loved it.

But she still hesitated for a second. She hadn't undressed in front of anybody for so long. But this was Ethan: she trusted him.

She reached for the hem of her sweater and pulled it slowly over her head, shaking out her hair as it fell back down around her.

"Better?"

Ethan's gaze traced a hot path over her belly, her breasts, lingered on her collarbones, and eventually met her eyes with a burning intensity. He dropped his head with a groan, and brushed the hair back from her face, dropping kisses on her cheeks, her lips, her neck, on every inch of exposed skin.

Abby moaned and tried to reach his belt buckle, still desperate to continue her exploration of his body. But with Ethan heavy on top of her, she couldn't reach. With one hand, she cupped his face and pulled it up to her own; kissed him hard as her other hand slipped between them.

Ethan laughed throatily in her ear and lifted his hips. "You know that would be a lot easier if..." He wrapped his arms tight around her waist and turned them over so that she straddled him.

And that was when she saw it.

The little red light.

Chapter Eight

Abby froze.

Ethan's hands were at her waist, trying to pull her down to him, but she pushed them away. Covering her chest with her arms, she climbed down from the couch and grabbed her sweater from the floor. She turned away from the bookshelf and pulled it over her head, hoping, more than anything, that she was wrong.

"Abby…?" He hadn't worked it out yet, didn't know that she knew. And then he followed her gaze to the shelf, and the video camera only half hidden there. "Oh my God. Abby, I promise you, this isn't as bad as it looks. It's not what you think."

She said nothing.

Instead, she walked over to the shelf, picked up the video camera, and sat in the armchair.

She checked the screen and confirmed that it was recording. That's when the tears started again.

Ethan hurried over to her and tried to take her into his arms, desperately trying to explain.

"Abby, I swear, I just wanted to record you reading the scene. I completely forgot that it was still on. I didn't know that…"

It didn't matter. He had lied to her.

What would he have done with the film, even if it were just her reading the scene? That performance was meant for him, and only him. As far as she was concerned that was every bit as intimate as what had come after, and what was going to happen after that. She pushed Ethan away and ran out of the room. She had to get out of here.

She slammed the door to her bedroom shut, turned the lock, and leaned back against it. Ethan was close behind her on the stairs, and she covered her ears with her hands to block out him trying to talk to her through the door.

What had she been thinking? She had walked into exactly the same mistake as she had two years before. How could she even think that she could trust him? She had known from the word go that he had been trying to manipulate her; he had got her exactly where he wanted her.

Thank God it hadn't gone any further. Who knows what he might have caught on camera. She had to get that file. Shit, why hadn't she just deleted it? It was a digital camera, so she had to worry about the memory cards, but was it wirelessly connected to a computer as well? Could she ever be sure that the files were really gone? At least she knew exactly what had been filmed. Why hadn't she brought the camera up here? In the shock she'd just wanted to get away, but she should have grabbed it. Ethan could have done anything with it by now.

He's not doing that, she reasoned with herself, *he's standing outside the door.* She would have to go and get the camera, delete the file, find out from Ethan whether it had been copied anywhere else. But that would mean talking to him, and she wasn't sure how she could even look at him after what he'd done.

She walked into the bathroom and shut the door. Through the two doors she could barely hear Ethan shouting to her from the landing. What would he think of her reaction? Any woman would be shocked to find herself being filmed—right? Anyone would react in the same way as she had—there was nothing there that would give her away. As long as she didn't have to talk to him, she might be able to get away without him finding out any more.

But of course she would have to talk to him. She was in his house, and more importantly, she had damage limitation to think about. Now wasn't the time to fall apart. She would talk to him for long enough to get rid of the files and tell him that she was leaving.

Abby took a deep breath and tried to compose herself. She had cried all over him once this evening, but she had no intention of a repeat performance. In fact, the tears that had started downstairs had dried up, and she was left with a burning anger. So. She needed a plan. Short and sharp: deal with the files, take the car—not to keep of course, she would have to arrange with Thomas to have it collected—and then what? It didn't matter what the police said, she knew she could never feel safe in that apartment again. It would have to be Candy's floor until she could find something else. She was suddenly well aware that she had not looked at a single apartment since she'd been staying here. So Candy's tonight, and apartment hunting first thing in the morning. She might not be able to find a palace, but she would find something.

First things first. She started gathering toiletries; with no time for any sort of order, she swept the whole lot into a bag, walked into the bedroom, and threw them into her suitcase. Ethan had obviously got tired of trying to talk to her through the door; she couldn't hear anything from the landing. She opened wardrobe doors, pulled everything off the hangers, and dumped them into her case.

When she was sure that she had everything from her rooms, she dragged the suitcase to the door, mentally reviewing the house, but there was nothing she'd need to come back for. She grabbed the door handle, but stopped herself from just throwing the door open.

She slammed her hand against the doorframe, trying to get her rising anger under control. What she really wanted to do was go down there and rage at him. Years' worth of anger was bubbling dangerously close to the surface, but she had to keep focused. If she gave in to the overwhelming urge to scream at him, she wouldn't get what she needed—the files deleted, and her out of here. This was never going to work if she couldn't calm down. And much as she would love to see Ethan Walker with a black eye right now, it wasn't part of the plan.

She needed a game face.

You are playing a calm, controlled, collected woman who is definitely not about to give in to fury. You are going to go downstairs and get the job done. Most importantly, you are not going to let Ethan Walker talk to you. If he talks, he'll manipulate you.

She set her shoulders back and walked out of the bedroom, to find Ethan sitting on the tiled floor outside, head in hands, with the camera beside him. He looked up at her as she walked out. At least he had wiped his usual self-confident smirk off his face, she thought. He had the grace to look sorry. Though he could just be pissed that he didn't get his way with her.

"Abby, I don't know what to say. I'm sorry, I completely forgot the camera was on."

Abby wanted to scream that the camera should never have been there in the first place. But, *Rule number one,* she told herself. Do not let him talk. Do not enter into conversation. If she couldn't physically shut him up, she would just pretend that he hadn't spoken.

"I want the camera."

"Abby, just let me explain."

"The camera."

She held out her hand as one would to a naughty child and wouldn't meet his eyes. She scrolled though the menus, found the file, and deleted it. She wished she had done this straight away. He had had plenty of time to make a copy, maybe even to email it. He could have been live-streaming the whole bloody affair on the internet for all she knew. *Too late now though,* she thought. She would just have to deal with what she could here and now.

"Are there any files on your computer?"

"No." Ethan sounded surprised.

"Have you sent files to anyone else?"

"Abby, of course not. What do you think…"

She threw him a look that told him *exactly* what she thought of him.

"I wish you'd just let me explain."

Abby held up a hand. *Rule number one.* She walked downstairs, through the kitchen, and out the back door. She raced towards her car as fast as she could while dragging her suitcase over the gravel. She just had to get out of here before…too late. A hand on her shoulder told her that Ethan had caught up with her.

"Come back inside."

"Why?" She turned to face him, shrugging his hand from her shoulder. "Whatever it is you want to say, I don't want to hear it."

"You have to know I didn't mean that to happen. Filming us that way I mean."

She suppressed the urge to scream, channeling her anger into heaving the case into the boot of the car. "You had a camera. You were recording me. What did you think would happen?" *What's happened to rule number one?* She was engaging him in conversation, exactly what she swore she wouldn't do.

"I did, but not for that, I just wanted to—"

She slammed the boot shut, sadly missing all of Ethan's fingers. "Forget it. I told you. I can't believe I've been so stupid again."

"Abby, please don't leave like this. If you would just listen to me, I can explain." That was the problem, she thought. Ethan could talk his way out of, or in to, anything. A week with him had compromised her more than anything had in the past two years. She opened the driver's side door and slid into the seat.

"Abby?"

"Ethan, listen to me. I am leaving now and I never want to see you again. Can I be any more clear?"

She stuck the car into drive and pulled away, scrabbling round in the door pocket for the beeper that would open the gate. As she pulled out of the driveway, she thought she saw a shadow cast by her headlights, but before she had a chance to wonder what it might be, the car was filled with the unmistakable white light of a flashbulb.

Chapter Nine

She banged on Candy's door again. Candy had definitely said she wasn't going out tonight, but Abby had been standing here with her suitcase at her feet for at least ten minutes, with no answer. Abby shivered.

Finally, the door in front of her flew open, and Candy stood in the doorway.

"Where's the fire?"

The anger of being woken faded quickly from her face as she took in Abby, tears threatening again now, and her suitcase.

"What happened?"

"Candy, I think I've done something really stupid."

• • •

Candy placed a steaming cup of coffee on the table beside her and then sat in the corner of the sofa opposite Abby. As soon as Abby had got here last night, she'd just crashed. Too much had happened, and her brain had just needed time to shut down and not think for a while. But it had been startlingly clear to Abby when she'd woken today that she couldn't go on as she had been. She had been stupid to think that she'd be able to keep her hiding out at Ethan's a secret. After last night, that wasn't an option—if she had been photographed, and she was pretty sure she had been, then it was surely only a matter of time before she was exposed. She needed help.

Whichever way she looked at it, she couldn't see any way that Candy might be trying to exploit her. Of all the people she had met in LA, she was the only one who didn't seem to want a piece of her. She was the only person that could help. Abby decided to start at the beginning, and for once, she would tell the truth.

"Candy, I don't really know where to start. There's a lot I haven't told you about me."

"Well I know that much at least..."

Abby was worried that Candy resented the secret that she'd been keeping, but when she looked up she saw only encouragement, no sign of criticism, on her friend's face.

"Well I guess the first thing to tell you is that I'm an actress, or at least I was. Back in England I had a regular part on a soap and I suppose I was pretty well known over there. After a couple of years I decided to come over to LA for a while, and see if I could make the jump to movies."

Candy nodded, taking the revelations in her stride. Abby guessed from the look on her face that she already had a hundred questions she was dying to ask, but she was managing to keep quiet so far.

"Anyway, my agent was supportive, so I quit my job, got new headshots done, booked my flights, arranged some initial meetings with casting agents. I thought this was it. I was really going to make a go of it." Abby could still remember the butterflies she'd had those first few days in LA. The few meetings she went to had gone well, or at least she had thought so. By the time she should have been hearing back she had cut off all communication with anyone who knew her. She guessed that now she would never know.

"My mother was mortified, of course. She thought—still thinks—that LA is a dreadful place. She's still of the mindset really that an actress is not much more than a prostitute, and no one more so than an aspiring actress in Hollywood.

"I'd been here less than a fortnight when I made a huge mistake. I met this guy at an industry party, he said he was a casting agent, gave me his card, and told me to drop by. I did some research and he seemed legit. Anyway, to cut a long story short—" Despite her determination to tell the truth, she couldn't bear to go through the finer details of her degradation. "There are photos of me… compromising photos. They've never been published, but I'm afraid something happened last night that means that they will."

"Are you going to tell me what happened?"

Abby took a deep breath; this was where Candy would have to show her true colors. If she wasn't the person that Abby hoped she was, she could be on the phone to a magazine newsroom within minutes.

"Well, this guy I've been staying with, I told you we had a mutual friend back home? We got…close. And then last night we had an argument, and I left, and I think I was photographed leaving his place."

"Why would someone be photographing you? Do you think they know about the photos?" Candy looked puzzled, trying to connect the dots, not realizing how much Abby was still holding back.

"Not yet. At least I hope not. But this guy, he's quite well known, and if they start digging around, trying to find out who I am—"

A cell phone rang with a shrill whistle from the other side of Candy's front door and Abby stopped abruptly.

She stared at the door for a moment, confused, and then in a split second realized what it must mean. She crossed the room in a few strides and threw the door open, knowing who she would find on the other side of it.

"Ethan, what the hell are you doing here?"

He stood in the hallway, phone in hand. "I had to talk to you. I'm sorry, it never seemed like quite the right time to…"

"So how much did you hear?"

"I can't believe you didn't tell me."

"Why should I tell you? I barely know you. How the hell did you even know I was here? No, don't tell me. That detective you hired."

An uncharacteristically subtle cough from Candy reminded Abby that she and Ethan weren't alone. She had been so angry when she had seen him that she'd forgotten that she hadn't quite got round to the details of the Ethan part of the story yet.

"Abby, what's going on?" Candy tried to peer through the doorway, but Ethan saved her the trouble, pushing past Abby and stepping into the room.

"I'm Ethan," he introduced himself to Candy, but Abby moved to stand in front of him, preventing him from coming any further.

"He's leaving," Abby assured Candy. "I'll explain everything when he's gone."

"Ethan Walker? This is the 'quite well-known' guy you've been crashing with?"

"He's leaving," Abby said again, turning towards Ethan. "I can't believe that after what you did," she spat, "that you can come in here and expect me to even *look* at you. Just get out."

"It's not as simple as that."

It never was. "Why not?"

"I am not going anywhere, because of this." He produced a newspaper from the back pocket of his jeans and placed it on the table. There on page five, under the headline *Who's Ethan's Girl?* was Abby, driving away from his place last night. Thank God it wasn't a great shot: the photographer had just caught the side of her face, and her hair covered most of it. She certainly wouldn't have people coming up to her on the street asking her if it was her in the papers, but it might be enough if someone knew what they were looking for. "I think given what I just overheard, you might want to think about what this could mean. If you're connected to me, it could cause problems. I want to help."

"Help? Help how? You can't just make this all go away because it's an inconvenience for your little project," she railed at him.

Candy stepped around the pair of them warily. "Abby, I think I'm going to give you two time to talk." With her eyes, Abby begged her to stay. "Don't worry, I'll just be out in the corridor, but I think you guys need to talk." Her eyes flicked to the newspaper, and then back to Abby. "Yell if you need me."

As soon as Candy left the room, Ethan was straight down to business. "So this is why you wouldn't take the part?"

"I am not going over this again. If you have something to say about these pictures, say it, and then go. But just so that we're clear, I will never forgive you for what you did."

"Abby, I know what I did was bad, but, honestly, it's not as bad as you're thinking. I just wanted to be able to show you how good you are. I never meant to record anything else. I just forgot."

"How can you say that? What you did, Ethan, just filming me in the first place, was terrible. I trusted you. I've not trusted anyone in such a long time, and now I remember why. I knew from the start that getting involved with you was a bad idea, but you had to push it, had to keep pushing. And then you film me, doing…what we were doing. I just want you to go."

Ethan looked shocked at her words.

"I want to help, if I can." He reached a hand towards her, but Abby crossed her arms over her body. She'd let him close once before, but she wouldn't be stupid enough to do it again.

"There's nothing you can do."

"You keep saying that, but it's not true. I'll speak to my lawyer. My press team. I can get them to lay a false trail, get them to make up a girlfriend, say you were delivering from a restaurant. I don't know, we'll think of something. The other stuff might be more difficult, but we can sort that too. You're not the first person this has happened to, the first person to make this mistake. Photos can be made to disappear. Photographers, journalists, newspapers can all be persuaded around to my point of view. I can make all of that happen. Just tell me you want me to do it."

She'd never seen Ethan look like this before—anxious, restless. But she wasn't fooled. He wasn't sorry for hurting her; he just knew that there was no way he could ever get her to change her mind about the film after what he'd done. And there was no way that she would tell him the truth. How could she lay bare her most painful memories when he'd practically recreated them last night?

"Right, and what's the catch?"

"There is no catch. Let me help you. You can't go on as before, and these pictures from last night, they're a way for someone to find you, if that's what you think they want to do."

He was right, of course. She had no doubt that the people that attacked her, tricked her, assaulted her, would be monitoring their investment. If they weren't then the photos would have appeared by now. No, they were biding their time, waiting, looking out for any sign that her Hollywood career might be on the up. Now that she'd been photographed leaving Ethan Walker's home looking decidedly disheveled, finding out who she was, was already at the top of someone's to-do list.

"Tell me exactly what you're suggesting."

"Let me take care of this. Do you even realize that there are companies who specialize in this sort of thing? We have lots of options. I can make the photos go away."

Abby looked again at the newspaper. Running and hiding had worked for a while, but these photos changed everything. Doing nothing was no longer an option. And as much as she didn't want to have to put her future in Ethan's hands, she didn't know anyone else who could wield the sort of power he had. The sort that would be needed to make this disappear.

"I want this to go away. But I don't trust you." There was no point trying to sugar-coat it. She was finding it hard enough to be in the same room as him; she didn't want him more involved in this than he had to be. "If you could put me in touch with the people who can help…"

"I can, but Abby. I want to do this. Please. Let me."

What choice did she have? She couldn't make this go away without his help. She needed his contacts.

"Fine. I'll meet your lawyer."

• • •

What had he done?

How could he have been so stupid? In hindsight, he could see what a terrible idea it had been. He had just wanted to show her how good she was, how good he knew she was, thinking that maybe then she would reconsider his offer. He would do anything to take that back, to have her look at him like she did yesterday morning. To see her glowing when he looked at her, rather than burning with anger. She wouldn't even look him in the eye now.

He couldn't begin to think about what this meant for the movie. In a way, things were better. He finally knew what the problem was, why Abby kept saying no; and, as he'd known all along, it was nothing that he couldn't take care of. He could fix this. But then what? He still had no assurance that Abby would make the movie. If anything, he was further away than he had ever been.

He'd been shocked to overhear what she told Candy. He knew that young actresses made these mistakes all the time—it wasn't that unusual—and he could see why Abby might be embarrassed. But he knew that she was still holding out on him. When he looked in her eyes, he could see there was something she wasn't telling him, a side to all of this that he didn't understand yet. But at least now he knew part of it. All he had to do was set things in motion with his lawyers and he could make this right. Maybe, then, she might be able to look at him again without so obviously wanting to spit at him.

Chapter Ten

Abby sat in the plush reception area of the offices of Henderson, Jones, and Thompson, biting her cuticles and waiting for her appointment with Joel Henderson, Ethan's lawyer. Henderson was running twenty minutes late, and it wasn't helping her nerves. She'd called as soon as Ethan had given her his details, and spent a good couple of hours on the internet, Googling him and his practice, trying to find any evidence of anything that wasn't completely above board.

She, of all people, knew that this wasn't a fail-safe method. But with the internet not showing anything to suggest he was out to exploit her, what choice did she have? Ethan had backed her into a corner weeks ago, and this was the only way she could see out of it.

Just as she was thinking that she would have to go and ask the receptionist how much longer she would be waiting, a short man in his fifties, his face lined from too much sun and his hair grey at the temples, approached her. Mr. Henderson, she assumed.

"Sorry we're running a bit late, Miss Smith, but Mr. Walker has just called me from downstairs. He'll be here any minute, so we can go right ahead and get started."

"I'm sorry, we were waiting for Ethan?"

Mr. Henderson's face showed his confusion. "You didn't know..."

"I didn't know he'd be joining us," Abby said through gritted teeth, hesitant to let a stranger know how strong—and conflicted—her feelings about Ethan were.

The two days that she'd spent away from him had done nothing to soften her anger. Whatever his reasons were, and regardless of whether he knew what had happened to her, filming her had been a gross violation of her privacy. But although her anger hadn't faded, other thoughts seemed to be squeezing around the edges of it, reminding her of what had been happening just before she'd spotted the camera, and what would inevitably have happened if she hadn't spotted it in time. It was as if Ethan had split into two people in her mind. The one she couldn't stop herself hating, and the one she couldn't stop herself mentally undressing. Fortunately it was the former who stepped out of the lift into the sleek lobby. Anger was easier for her to handle right now than desire. She knew where she stood with anger. Ethan must have spotted the look on Abby's face before he reached her.

"Joel, could I have a few moments with Miss Smith in private before we get started?"

"Sure, use my office. I'll be through in a few minutes."

Abby waited until the door was shut behind them. This firm had been hired to protect her interests, but that didn't mean that she had to trust them. Proof of that was standing right in front of her.

"What are you doing here?"

"I assumed you knew I'd be here?" He was meant to be helping her. He wasn't meant to be running the whole show.

"Why would I assume that? Your message said that I would be meeting your lawyer here. You never said that you'd be coming."

"I thought I was sorting this out for you. I want to help. I can help more if I'm here. Do you want me to leave?"

"Of course I want you to leave. Are you going to?"

"Not unless you make me."

Abby considered her options. She needed his help—and that would be easier if he stayed. Joel was probably going to tell him everything anyway—he was paying the bills, after all.

• • •

Joel straightened his papers as he summed up everything they had covered over the last hour. The photos of Abby outside Ethan's couldn't be hidden now, but Joel had outlined what they were doing to make sure that there were no further invasions into Ethan's privacy, and that other than the small chance that someone recognized, beyond doubt, the back of her head, there would be no way of finding her. They'd concocted some cover story of an assistant from the studio dropping off a script. Though the car was registered to Ethan, it was easy enough to spin it into it being a pool car.

"And so I'm afraid this is going to be the more difficult part, Miss Richards," Joel said. "I understand that there are some photographs from your past that you are worried about being published. While there are no guarantees, we have had some success in cases like this before. Not related to Mr. Walker in any way," he clarified quickly. "So if I can ask you some questions about what happened, I'm hopeful that we can ensure no one sees these pictures."

Abby nodded.

"Start from the beginning. How did you meet the photographer? Did you approach him, or did he approach you?"

Abby shuddered, thinking of when he had first approached her at the party. Why hadn't her alarm systems sounded? She thought back to how different she must have been then, to assume that he was everything he said that he was. Now she couldn't imagine being naive enough to fall for his tricks. "So you met this man at a party—can you remember what the event was?"

She tried to answer his questions as honestly as she could, without revealing more than she wanted to about her situation. She couldn't change what had been done to her, but having been exposed so totally, so cruelly, she'd fiercely protected herself ever since. Deciding exactly how much of herself she wanted to share, and with whom. But now, because of Ethan pulling at little threads, the whole story seemed to be falling apart. She needed something she could hold back, that she could control.

"Yes, but I've given you his name, and the address of the offices. Is that not enough information?"

"You're absolutely right, it should be. But you never know. Sometimes people change their name, for legitimate reasons or not, and they move about for plenty of reasons. If he's not at the address you told us, I want to make sure that we can find him, without having to ask you to come in and see us again."

Joel continued to pick away at her memories. Teasing out another detail here, another clue there. She spent an age considering her every answer, and she could see Ethan watching her, trying to work out why she was being evasive when she'd finally told him what he wanted to know. *Let him wonder,* she thought. *He wouldn't even know this much if he hadn't been eavesdropping.*

She was still angry with him. How could she not be after what he'd done? But he did look contrite. In fact, she'd not seen him looking this troubled in the time that she'd known him. No doubt more to do with the latest problems with the movie than with losing her though. Personally, at least. She'd never been more than just another actress to him. And though it might have been working in reverse, the sofa in his study had been no more than a casting couch. That he would compromise so much, just to try and get her to agree to the movie, showed where his true loyalties lay. She just wished he didn't have to look so bloody good when he was worried.

Big, confident, get-things-done Ethan was hot. More than hot. She'd not been able to resist him, after all. But Ethan with just a hint of self-doubt, a hint of remorse…that was worse. How could she hate him and want to make him feel better at the same time?

When Joel felt that he had sufficiently picked apart her memories, and she had laid as little as she thought she could get away with on the table, he began to gather up his notes.

"I don't think we'll have anything to tell you immediately, but I'm hoping that we'll be able to make sure the photos are in safe hands in a matter of weeks," he said. "As long as you two manage to keep your meetings secret, then there's no reason we can't start talking about the contract."

Abby felt a shudder go through her. There it was—the catch. "What contract?" she demanded icily.

Joel looked from Abby to Ethan, seeming to realize his mistake.

"I'm sorry, I seem to have spoken too soon. I…" He collected his papers and bolted for the door, aware of what a touchpaper he'd just lit. "I think I'll leave you two to talk. Again."

Abby waited until he had left the room before she spoke.

"Are you going to tell me that there's been some sort of mistake? You have no idea what Joel's talking about?"

"No. Abby, I wasn't going to bring this up yet, actually, but I thought, if we can get the photos sorted … You have said all along that it's not that you don't want to make the film…"

Back to reality. In the time since Ethan had left Candy's room, there had been the occasional moment when she'd allowed herself to think about the last few days that she had spent at Ethan's place and how close they had gotten, or she thought they had at any rate. And she'd started to let a small part of herself believe that he was doing this to make it up to her. To show her that he cared. That he was doing all of this for her, not because of what he wanted from her. But of course his help came at a price.

She crossed her arms across her body. "So you're going to help me get rid of the photos, but only if I take the role in your picture. Am I right?"

Nothing had changed from that first night when he'd manipulated her into agreeing to come to his house. He always got what he wanted, whatever it cost. This was just another business expense for him. *She* was just another business expense for him.

"No. It's not like that at all. But once I have this sorted, then why wouldn't you agree? It's what you've said you wanted all along."

It struck her that she meant less to Ethan than his women usually did. And for Ethan Walker that was saying something. He had always seen her as just an actress; a commodity. Their time together in his house had been just one long seduction campaign; he had clearly hoped that if he could get her into his bed, he could get her to agree to the movie.

"I bet you were pleased, weren't you, when you overheard me at Candy's? All this time you've been wondering how to get me to agree, and now I hand it to you on a plate."

Ethan shook his head, but didn't deny it.

Wasn't this how he had always worked? Grand gestures and gifts that were quickly followed by a reminder of what he wanted. It was the tea chest all over again. It was promising to leave the diner as long as she agreed to go to his house. It's not that she wasn't grateful. Of course she was. And given time she was pretty sure that she would have agreed to do the movie anyway. She'd wanted to be able to say yes all along. But until she felt this despair, knowing how he really thought of her, she hadn't realized the strength of her own feelings for Ethan, or been so certain that they weren't reciprocated.

Now she could see the reason she'd felt so betrayed when she'd seen that red light.

She was in love with him. But he didn't love her.

She'd only ever been a project to him. A challenge.

Even though this meeting raked through things she never wanted to talk about again, she had had the occasional moment where she'd let herself think that this might be it. This might be what fixed her future. After this, she wouldn't have to hide anymore.

And now Ethan was going to make her choose. She could do what he wanted—accept his help, live out her childhood dreams, and acknowledge what she'd suspected for some time now: that she was nothing more than a product to be dressed and undressed, and kissed and dropped, and hired at will. Or she could go back to her life at the diner, living in fear of exposure.

"Fine. I'll do it."

• • •

Ethan was still sitting at Joel's desk when the lawyer walked back into the office.

"Miss Smith has left I take it?"

"She has. I thought it best that I stay awhile before I go; I wouldn't want anyone to connect us this way, not until I can be sure that we've got these pictures contained."

"So she agreed? You really should have told me that you'd not spoken to her about the contract," he admonished. "That was hardly fair on either of us."

Ethan wasn't listening. She'd agreed. He'd known all along that she would eventually, of course. He was never going give up. But he hadn't expected her to say yes today.

"So was she happy with the contract terms? Do you want to talk through any changes now?"

Ethan shook his head. They hadn't talked about terms; she hadn't even asked what she'd be paid. But even though she'd agreed, and he finally had what he wanted—there was nothing stopping his film now—he didn't feel as elated as he thought he would.

"No, she said she needed to call her agent. They haven't spoken for a long time. And anyway, we need to deal with these pictures before we can even think about moving on with the contract."

Ethan was thinking through next steps in his head, but he didn't have the rush of excitement he'd been expecting. He'd been prepared for the adrenaline he normally got when he pulled off a difficult project. The exhilaration of knowing that the movie was really going to be made. But he just felt…flat. Abby was angry with him. He'd thought that she might have started to calm down now—after all, he was doing everything he could to fix this—but she had barely even looked at him today.

"Is there something wrong?" Joel asked.

"You may have noticed things are a little…strained with Miss Richards and me. I would rather we were on better terms than this before we start working together. But it's nothing for you to worry about." He hated the way she wouldn't even look at him; nothing could punish him more. And they couldn't work together like this. He couldn't even negotiate a contract with her if they weren't speaking at all. "I ought to be going. Thanks again for this, Joel, and I know I don't have to say again how important it is that this remains confidential."

He needed to make things right between him and Abby if they were going to have a good working relationship. That was it, he convinced himself. That was the only reason for the gnawing sensation in his gut.

And then, once she was speaking to him, perhaps they could … He stopped that line of thought instantly. He'd gotten what he needed—she was doing the movie. He had to let that be enough. He'd taken too big a risk, getting involved with her personally, and it had nearly backfired. He shuddered slightly as he considered how close he had come to losing her—the end of his career had been so close he could practically taste it for the past few days. He couldn't risk the project falling apart.

Chapter Eleven

Abby sat in her trailer on their first day of shooting trying to calm her nerves. She'd thought she might feel a little more confident being back on home soil, but so far the opposite was true. Three months had passed since she last saw Ethan, but only now was it hitting home that her hiding was over. Back here, she wasn't Abigail Smith: Abigail Smith could hide away in a diner, keeping out of trouble.

In Britain she was Abby Richards: national sweetheart, tabloid fodder, and—she felt slightly sick at the thought—daughter of Rosemary Smith. She'd managed to put off seeing her mother so far, but she knew that it could only be delayed so long.

Here she was, her first day of shooting on location in Surrey, about to star in a huge production, and she was sitting on her hands to stop herself nibbling on her cuticles. The next big Hollywood star—at least that's what the papers were calling her—was driving herself crazy with nerves. The biggest moment in her career was around the corner; she was risking the humiliation and violation of graphic and explicit photographs of herself being published even with everything that Joel had done over the past three months. She was certain that she would have to see her mother at least once; and there was only one person on this whole shoot who believed that she was good enough to do this. It wasn't her.

• • •

The last time she'd seen Ethan he'd turned up at the diner with no warning. Candy had burst through the door into the kitchen, looking nervous.

"Ethan's here."

"*Here* here?" Abby felt the old panic starting to rise.

"As in standing at the counter, asking for you, here."

Shit—would he never learn? How many times did she have to tell him that they had to keep these things quiet, well away from where anyone knew her? She could feel her pulse start to quicken and the color rise up her face as the familiar feeling of anger, now tinged with disappointment and disillusionment, swept through her body.

She pushed past Candy and into the diner, fully prepared to give Ethan hell, again, for turning up at her work like this.

But the mere sight of him, when combined with a racing pulse and flushed face, was giving certain parts of her anatomy other ideas.

He was leaning against the counter, tapping away on his BlackBerry, and hadn't noticed her arrive. She looked him up and down, slowly, and wished that she hadn't. Her treacherous body didn't seem to care that she was angry with him. It seemed intent on reminding her of all the reasons she'd liked him in the first place.

He pushed a hand through his hair, and must have caught sight of her out of the corner of his eye. He did a double take, and then looked her right in the eye.

Abby tried to look away, knew that she should, but faced with the heat in Ethan's eyes, she couldn't. She knew that look. She knew exactly what it meant when his eyes softened and the ghost of a smile played around the corner of his mouth. He wanted her. Her stomach clenched with a shot of desire, and she forced herself to remember what he had done.

"Ethan, you can't be here." She stepped around the counter, her arms folded, and prepared to frog march him out of there.

Her sharp words didn't seem to dent his mood. Instead, a full-blown smile spread across his features. "Actually, I can be. I am."

"You know what I mean. You have to go. Now."

His smile spread further. Abby pointedly looked away, determined that she wouldn't let her attraction to him make her forget what was important.

"No. I'm here to tell you that you officially no longer have to worry about that. We can be completely out in the open. I just spoke to Joel. It's over." The blood that had been racing around Abby's body seemed to still. Her face paled, and she leaned back against the counter. She'd dreamt about this moment so many times, but she'd never actually thought that this could happen. That it could actually be over.

She could barely form the words, but she had to know this was real.

"You're absolutely certain? No more photos? How can you be sure?"

Ethan reached for her hand and pulled her towards him. "We can never be a hundred per cent certain." He looked down and met her eye. "Unfortunately that's just the way things are with digital files. But we were very thorough. My contact, um…'accessed' all of the computers in the office you went to, as well as laptops and a remote network, and did a whole load of other stuff that I don't really understand. But it comes down to this: he got rid of everything that he could find. He's also scoured the internet, to see if they had been shared with anyone, but he doesn't think that happened. I trust him. So the only copies are now in our possession. Joel's got to keep hold of them for now, just until he wraps up some paperwork, but then they're yours to do what you want with."

Abby opened her mouth to speak, but couldn't form the words. Her life had been ruled by her need to hide, to protect herself. What was she meant to do now that that was gone? She didn't even know how to begin thinking about this.

And what about Ethan? She wasn't going to forget what he'd done. She couldn't. But now he was standing in front of her looking so bloody pleased, and hot, and…he had done this. If he'd never filmed her, pushed her, then how long would she have spent hiding here? Months? Years? It hurt, knowing that to Ethan she had just been something that he needed for his film. But it was hard to be upset, knowing that he was the one who had given her her life back. And harder still when her body seemed determined to rebel against her.

The slow circles that his thumb had started making around her palm were making it difficult for her to think, and still Ethan seemed determined not to let her look away. Slowly, the knowledge that she was free from everything that she'd been frightened of was seeping through her brain, and she could feel the delight spreading through her body. It was really over.

She waited for Ethan to mention the contract. They'd discussed it only briefly before; surely he'd want to pin her down to specific terms and conditions.

"I have to get back to the office." Ethan broke the stunned silence his announcement had brought. "I just wanted to be the one to tell you." He leaned in and kissed her cheek, the pressure of his lips against her skin lasting just long enough to make her want more. And then he was walking away from her and out the door. That was the last time she'd spoken to him.

He'd called at least once a day for the first week after that, but somehow she couldn't quite seem to press the answer button. She wasn't purposefully avoiding him; was just building up her courage. And by the time she got there, he'd stopped calling. It was a good thing, she told herself. It had only taken a week for him to lose interest, to find someone else to share dinner and laughs with. She'd studiously avoided magazines and newspapers, knowing that the sight of him with some young starlet on his arm would cut her.

If only the ache that had taken up residence in her chest after she'd last seen him had faded with time, she might have a chance of getting over him. But instead it had grown with every day that went past. She'd spoken to Joel about disposing of the photos for good. Her agent had handled the contract negotiation for the movie, and so she'd managed to make it all the way here, to England, to the set, to Ethan's dream of a movie, without exchanging another word with him.

• • •

She'd been waiting all morning for the knock on her trailer door that would tell her that Ethan was here, but so far there had been nothing. Everything had been done in such a hurry and, with Ethan characteristically getting what he wanted, she was cast and signed and contracted before anyone else on the movie had had a say. Maybe she should be out there trying to get to know her colleagues, but she just didn't feel comfortable. She had nothing to hide anymore, but that didn't make trying to get to know people feel any less strange after years of trying to be invisible.

There was a knock on the door and her heart started racing.

She'd been expecting it all morning—he'd have to come and talk to her before everything kicked off, but the anticipation just made the effect stronger. She took a deep breath as she opened the door. It didn't work. He smiled at her and the walls seemed to close in. As he pushed past her into the trailer, she realized she had no idea how to react to him now. She couldn't shout and rage, not when he'd solved the complete mess she'd found herself in, and, technically speaking, she supposed he was her boss now.

But she couldn't forget that he'd hurt her either. And, more depressingly, she didn't seem to be able to forget everything that had happened before he'd hurt her. She clenched her hands into fists at her side. She had never had to think about what to do with them before, but now, in this confined space with Ethan, they seemed monstrously awkward. How could she have forgotten how hands normally behaved? She clasped them behind her back before they did something stupid.

"Hi." It seemed an inadequate word to express the tumult of emotions she was experiencing, but she couldn't seem to think of anything witty or sophisticated to express her conflicting, flip-flopping thoughts.

"Hey." As usual, Ethan seemed completely at ease, obviously unaffected by what had happened between them before. It was funny, being trapped in this small space with Ethan, in such close proximity to a bed, that all Abby could think about was what had happened before.

She finally looked up, but darted her eyes away again quickly. She'd forgotten how intense his gaze was. And being reminded wasn't doing anything to help her calm down.

Oh, this whole "being professional" thing was going to be *so* much harder than she'd expected. And she had been expecting it to be almost impossible. Ethan was as relaxed and self-confident as ever. *But of course he is*, Abby thought to herself. What reason did he have to feel nervous or embarrassed? She'd already established that he didn't have strong feelings for her. She was business, a project, and he had her exactly where he wanted her.

"Are you okay?" Ethan asked, sensing her discomfort.

"Fine, just nerves," Abby replied, more sharply than she'd intended. She'd thought that seeing Ethan would dissolve all of the nerves and tension that she'd felt building over the months she'd spent waiting for filming to start, months of thinking about when she'd see him again. But now she realized how silly that was. When had being in the same room as Ethan ever made her feel calm?

"Don't be nervous," Ethan soothed automatically. "You're going to be great. I know that. Everyone out there knows that—"

"But that's just the thing, isn't it," Abby snapped. Ethan's words had hit a nerve. "*I* don't know that. And *they* definitely don't know that." Words started building up behind her tongue, and Abby knew that now she'd started, she wasn't going to be stopped easily. "You've just parachuted me into this project. I doubt anyone else even got a say, and now I've got to go out there and face them all, knowing what they must all think of me. And even if the photos don't ever come out, my reputation's still ruined, because I just walked into this job and every single person out there has guessed how. Everyone knows about us, and assumes that I just got this job by sleeping with you, which isn't as wide of the mark as I would like to think." Ethan stepped toward her with his hands out, palms facing her, as if approaching a wild horse, but she just couldn't stop. "And I haven't worked for years, and even when I was working, it was nothing like this, and, and…"

"Abby," Ethan said, very firmly, placing his hands on her shoulders, but not attempting to draw her close. "I want you to listen to me very carefully. Everyone working on this film knows exactly how good you are. I made them all watch the old footage of you, and they were as blown away as I was. That's why you've turned up here without meeting many of them. Trust me. There's too much riding on this for it to be just about what I want."

It made it easier for Abby that he was talking to her like this. Soothing her as he would any actress—there was no real intimacy in it. It helped to ground her, remind her that everything they had shared before…it wasn't a lie as such, he'd never said he had feelings for her, it's just that it hadn't been as serious for him as it was for her. Oh, he would probably be happy to fall into an affair, Abby thought, but she would always be just another actress, another part of his movie empire.

She couldn't do it. She mustn't let him draw her back in.

"So, I was thinking. We really need to catch up. Shall I book somewhere for dinner?"

Dinner, like a date? She took a step back from him, forcing his hands to slide off her shoulders.

"Ethan, that's really not a good idea."

"It's just dinner, work. I've a few ideas I want to run past you."

It was never that simple with Ethan. She'd thought she could get away with *just dinner* once before, and look how that had ended up. True, it was unlikely that they would be faced with a life-or-death shooting in leafy Surrey, but around Ethan she couldn't afford to take chances.

"Ethan, we're working together. And although I'm grateful for all…" She gestured around her, knowing he would understand. He'd helped her get here; get out of the hole that she'd dug herself in LA. "It doesn't change what happened before. I just need to keep things professional."

Chapter Twelve

Ethan watched Abby as she loaded her tray; she kept her head down, her blonde waves falling across her face like a curtain, blocking her from his and everyone else's view, and headed straight to an empty table at the far end of the catering tent. As she had every day for the past few days, she sat with her back to everyone, as far away as possible from any of their colleagues, even the ones she had known before she came out to LA. He recognized the way she was carrying herself. This was Abby in hiding, afraid, and it had to stop.

He walked up to her table and pulled out a chair, folding himself into it before she had a chance to argue. "Mind if I sit here?"

Abby sighed, and Ethan knew that of course she minded. She'd been avoiding him for days. Unless it was strictly work-related—of course, she was ever the professional—she just wanted to be left alone. She was never rude, never anything but perfectly polite and cordial. But the shutters in her eyes that he'd seen lift, a tiny fraction at a time, in LA, had slammed back down. And she wasn't just keeping him out, it was everyone.

"If you must."

"What's with you today?" He was officially worried about her. He hated seeing her so unhappy. So far, her work had been fine, but there was a distance and awkwardness with her co-star, Matt, that was just visible on-screen. He needed her to relax. He needed her to connect with her colleagues, because if she kept putting this distance between herself and everyone else, it was going to start causing tension. This was supposed to be what she wanted. She'd been hiding out in that diner for years—surely she should be pleased that it was all over.

"I just don't think it's a good idea." She sighed. "Us sitting together like this. People might talk. I don't want any gossip." *Well, if you would just make an effort to get along with people, then this wouldn't even be an issue,* he thought. But she was the one too scared to even try and let anyone in.

"Abby, you know you don't have to worry about gossip. None of that matters."

"Everyone's watching us. They must think…"

Ethan glanced over her shoulder at the crowds of people milling around the tent, helping themselves to food and chatting, completely uninterested in this conversation. "Abby, no one is watching us. This isn't high school; no one cares who has lunch with whom. You don't think that you might be being just a little…" Abby raised her eyebrows, obviously willing him to finish that sentence. "Never mind."

He sighed. This was getting ridiculous. Okay, it's not like Abby was imagining things *completely*. There had been one or two people who had wondered how Abby had got this job without officially auditioning, and maybe they'd picked up on something in their body language and guessed that they had been…close. But those sorts of rumors were hardly unusual. They circulated about someone on pretty much every set, and everyone knew to take these things with a grain of salt. He certainly hadn't expected Abby to be taking it this seriously. He decided to change tack. "How are things working with Matt?"

"Fine," she said, noncommittally.

Ethan knew she'd met him briefly back in LA when they'd screen-tested. Ethan had been prepared to pull the plug on Matt's contract if the chemistry wasn't working, but even with a little tension from both sides, they had looked good on camera together.

Ethan brushed back the hair that Abby had let fall in front of her face, and tucked it behind her ear, touching her chin slightly to bring her face up and forcing her to meet his eyes. "You know, if you were eating with some of the others, then it wouldn't have to be just you and me." And if she was sitting with some of the others, she might not have a pout on her that made it impossible for him to sit anywhere else.

She looked over at the group sitting in the middle of the marquee laughing and joking together. Ethan studied her face as she watched them; he saw the doubt there, the hesitation. "Ethan, I'm not sure that I remember how. And what if they're talking about us?"

"Abby, I'm going to say this again, and I want you to actually listen this time. No one is talking about you. And even if they were, what would it matter? You and I both know that you got this job on merit. What does it matter what anyone else thinks?"

"Ethan, of course it matters. I don't want people thinking that I got this job just because I was willing to sleep with you." She checked over her shoulder that no one was listening, and lowered her voice to a whisper. "If that's what comes of this, then what was the point in me hiding all that time? What was the point of Joel getting rid of the pictures? These people, they might not actually be seeing me naked, but what does that matter? They're all thinking it. They're all thinking that I was willing to sell my body just to get this part. Everything that I've been worried about, everything that you, we, tried to stop happening. It's all happened anyway, hasn't it? My mother was right. This business, it's left me with no integrity. Whether it's true or not, to these people, I'm just a whore."

• • •

Ethan wouldn't understand. Even Marcus, her agent, thought that she'd only got the part because she'd slept with Ethan. The one person in this industry who was meant to be looking out for her, who was meant to be on her side, had just assumed that she was willing to drop her knickers to get what she wanted.

To say that Marcus had been surprised to hear from her was an understatement—she could still hear the shock in his voice when he'd answered the phone to her.

"Abby Smith? Abby *Richards*. The same Abby Richards that disappeared off the face of the planet months—no, years—ago? Who hasn't returned a single one of my calls? The Abby Richards whose *mother* I was reduced to calling, just to make sure you weren't dead in a gutter somewhere? Your *mother*, Abby."

She'd been worried that he would be angry, that he wouldn't agree to represent her. But any fears about that had been removed when she told him that she had a new contract in the bag, and he just had to negotiate terms with Ethan Walker. He wasn't going to walk away from that in a hurry.

"Ethan Walker? He called me about you, you know. I'd have given him your address if I'd had it, whether you wanted me to or not. Difficult man to say no to from what I've heard..." If only he knew. "So...Abby...is there anything I should know about?" Shit, he *did* know.

"What do you mean?"

"It's just you disappear for years, drop out of the business, and now you're cast as the lead in the film that's going to be the highlight of Ethan Walker's career."

"I know it looks a little odd..." She had to admit, it didn't look great.

"And you haven't screen tested at the studio."

"Not yet..." She didn't think that Ethan's surreptitious home video really counted. And even if it did, it wasn't something she was going to share with Marcus.

"And you've not even met the director of the picture."

"Right."

"Well, darling, how you got the part is none of my business. We might just want to be a teensy bit careful with how we present it in the press…we don't want you out there with a sordid reputation, do we? But enough time for that later."

• • •

Of course it mattered what people thought.

Abby left Ethan sitting at the table and went to fetch a cup of coffee, but hesitated as she turned to walk back. Should she go back and sit with Ethan, currently lounging back precariously in his chair looking outrageously tempting, or sit with the group who were giggling and gossiping together? *I suppose if I sit with them, it'll stop Ethan hassling me,* she thought. And going and sitting back with Ethan wasn't exactly going to quash any rumors anyway.

She'd never say it to his face, but perhaps there was something in what Ethan was saying. Okay, so they might gossip about her, but hiding away, especially if Ethan was determined to keep seeking her out, wasn't going to make it stop.

She took her coffee and a muffin and walked slowly over to the group at the table, but faltered when she saw there wasn't a chair free. She was just about to walk away when Molly, one of the girls from make-up, looked up and saw her.

"Abby, come sit down and settle an argument. You, Ryan Gosling, and Jude Law are the only three people left alive at the end of the world. Which do you choose to start repopulating the planet with?"

This was what they had been talking about? She could see from the way that the others eagerly awaited her answer that this conversation had been running for a while.

A chair seemed to appear from nowhere, and shoved into the back of her knees, forcing her to sit down. She glanced over her shoulder to see Ethan walking away from her, his face fixed determinedly forwards.

"Well..." she began, and seven pairs of eyes stared at her expectantly. She realized that Matt was also sitting at the table, and couldn't help wondering if he'd had an opinion. "Matt, who did you choose?"

"I abstained," he replied. "Neither of them are really my type." He gave her a pointed look.

Was he flirting with her? It had been a long time since she'd really flirted with anyone, except for Ethan of course. She shook her head slightly and focused on the question at hand.

"If I were to choose Jude Law, I suppose the whole population of the planet would be English, and, I don't know, maybe we'd be too polite or something to really thrive...so for the sake of genetic diversity...Ryan Gosling?"

A cheer erupted from one end of the table, it seemed she had cast the deciding vote, and Ryan Gosling was to become the father of all mankind.

• • •

Ethan shifted uncomfortably in his chair and checked his watch. Why the hell was this taking so long? The last take had looked great, he couldn't see anything wrong on the monitor at all, but still the director wanted to go for "just one more." He stuck his hands in his pockets before anyone could see his clenched fists. If he had to watch Abby kissing this guy one more time, he was going to go crazy.

He looked over to where she was getting her make-up touched up, and could see, even from this distance, that her lips were already red and puffy from the time she had spent kissing this idiot. Ethan had never had a problem with Matt before today. In fact, he'd been thrilled to sign him to the film, certain that his talent, name, and looks, would help to guarantee success for the picture. But from the minute he'd arrived on set this morning, he'd done nothing but irritate Ethan. Ethan watched as he walked over to talk to Abby, the make-up artist giving her a little tap on the nose when she turned to talk to him.

She looked so relaxed, Ethan thought, remembering how worried he'd been about her just a few weeks ago. But ever since he'd forced her into lunching with her colleagues, her confidence had grown, and now she shone whether the camera was on her or not.

He stifled a snarl as Matt reached out and smoothed one of Abby's curls. *If you hadn't been quite so enthusiastic about messing it up in the first place…*

He felt a twist of anxiety in his stomach. What was wrong with him? There was obvious chemistry between these two, and they certainly seemed to be getting along; it should be making him happy. The better their relationship off screen, the better it'd come across in the film. So why did he want to storm over there and tell him to back the hell off?

He'd thought about being close to Abby again since they'd got here. Sure, he'd hoped that once her anger had cooled a little, and she'd seen that he hadn't meant to hurt her, then maybe she'd want to pick up where they'd left off. But although she was at least talking to him, she hadn't given any hint that she wanted more than that.

This was unfinished business. That's what caused these little stabs of jealousy deep in his gut. He didn't like the thought that Matt would get to know Abby, really get to know her, in a way that he hadn't. Perhaps if he and Abby could just finish what they started in LA, then this feeling would be gone, and he could get on with things. Because if he could barely manage to sit and watch a couple of hours filming, how was he ever going to make this picture a success, even if they did get it finished? He levered himself out of the chair and went to grab a cup of coffee, though really just glad for the excuse not to have to watch Abby smiling up at that guy for another minute.

• • •

An hour later Ethan gritted his teeth together, praying that this would be the last take. From this angle all he could see of Abby was the back of her head. If he tried hard, really hard, he could make himself believe that it wasn't even her that he was watching, that it was some other actress. But a few seconds into this kiss, with the intensity mounting and Matt pulling her closer, Abby turned her head, and Ethan could kid himself no longer. Beneath Matt's clunky, lumbering hand, he could recognize the exact line of her jaw—he could see that extra sensitive spot that made her moan when he pressed his lips there. He glanced at the monitor, hoping that a different view would help, but then instantly wished that he hadn't.

The screen showed a close up—he could see Abby's long eyelashes shadowing her cheeks, and the curve of her bottom lip as she smiled into the kiss. When he glanced over at the real-life floor show, Matt's hand was casually making its way down Abby's side, brushing against her breast before resting possessively on her butt. Ethan could feel the heat rising out of the pit of his belly, up over his tightening chest and down his arm to his clenched fist, as he braced his body for a fight. There was no way he could stand back and watch while Matt…while Matt…*molested* his girl. He didn't care what the consequences were. He was going out there and he would break the guy's jaw unless he took his hands off her.

"Cut!"

One word from the director and Ethan looked down at his raised fist as if it belonged to someone else. He looked up and met

Abby's eyes, then saw her gaze drop and take in his fight-ready stance.

He turned and walked away, anger still rushing in his ears, before he did something he might regret. But instead of doing the sensible thing and heading towards his office, or his car, he found himself walking straight towards Abby's trailer, opening the door, and going inside.

He sat on the bench seat, waiting for her to arrive, and stood up when the door opened.

"Ethan, what are you doing here?" She rubbed her temple, clearly not happy to see him.

"Waiting for you." He kept his voice controlled, determined not to give in to his anger.

"Well, I gathered that. Why are you here?"

He wished he knew the answer to that.

"Good day at the office?" he asked. Abby's eyes narrowed.

"And what's that supposed to mean?"

"Just what I said—have you had an enjoyable day?" Why was he doing this to himself? He didn't need to know if she'd enjoyed it. He wanted to scrub the images out of his brain, not cement them in there by talking about it. But something was nagging at him. He needed to know that she hadn't liked it. That it wasn't really *her* that was kissing Matt. He needed to know … He wasn't sure what it was that he needed to know. But he had to find some way of excising this weird, sharp pressure in his chest, and picking away at where it hurt seemed like a good place to start.

"Ethan, you were there for most of it, watching. You know exactly what sort of day I've had."

"No, I know *what* you've been doing all day. My question was whether you enjoyed it. Did you?" *Please say no, please say no,* he thought.

"I tried not to think about it to be honest. Snogging a practical stranger in front of a load of other strangers isn't generally high on my list of things to do, but it was work. I knew it had to be done, I did it. Now, are you going to tell me what's going on?"

"Not until you answer my question, goddammit. Did you enjoy kissing Matt all day?"

"You know what?" Abby said. "I've spent the last two years serving burgers and fries. This wasn't the worst day's work I've ever done." The pain in his chest grew sharper. This was clearly a bad idea. Definitely making things worse, not better.

"Great, well, that's all I needed to know."

Ethan walked past her to head to the door, but Abby put out a hand to stop him.

"You're just walking off? Ethan, what the hell is going…"

The touch of her hand on his skin made the pressure in his chest expand until it was occupying his whole body. He needed Abby close to him. That would make this better. He pushed her back against the wall of the trailer with one hand, and with the other gently tilted her head up to meet him as his mouth came down on hers. The momentary hesitation in Abby's lips melted away, and he slanted his head to deepen the kiss, moaning as her mouth opened. He groaned. That was better. He could feel the tension leaching out of his body as she responded to him.

His hands went to her waist and pulled her close, then dropped to her butt, wanting to claim it back after Matt's hands had been there.

Abby broke away from him, gasping for breath. "Ethan, what the hell was that?"

Not the reaction I was looking for, he thought belligerently.

"What was it? It was a kiss. What, you didn't like it? Let me guess, you'd rather be kissing Matt."

"Is that what this is about? You don't like other people playing with your toys? You just want to mark your territory? Why don't you go all the way and piss up the side of my trailer?"

"That's not what I meant...I just...I didn't like seeing him like that, with his hands all over you."

What was she talking about, marking his territory? That wasn't it at all. He just wanted...needed ... He was frustrated. He hadn't had a single woman since the moment that he'd first laid eyes on Abby in that awful greasy diner, and he was frustrated. Watching the last girl he'd kissed making out with someone else had got him riled up. That was all. He wasn't jealous. She wasn't his.

"It was his job to have his hands all over me. It was my job to let him. And, in case you've forgotten, you're the one who's paying us to do it. You are the one who wanted me to take this job. You begged me—"

"I never begged." *Was she kidding?*

"You begged me, and tricked me, and blackmailed me into doing this, and now I'm here, what? You've changed your mind? Well, tough. You're just going to have to deal with it."

• • •

Abby took a deep breath, not quite believing that the words had left her lips. Thoughts of Ethan kissing her had been haunting her more than she liked to admit. She'd kept her distance from him for the last couple of weeks, and once she'd started building friendships with her colleagues, he'd found it harder and harder to get her alone.

Her heart still stuttered at the occasional flashback to their time together at his place. And she'd woken more than once in an unladylike sweat after a *very* unladylike dream. But he was her boss. He wanted nothing more from her than to make his pet project happen, and maybe a convenient shag; she'd told herself time and time again that she wasn't prepared to settle for so little.

But when he'd kissed her, all such thoughts left her, as she remembered the joy of being so close to him, the bliss of being in his arms, pressed up against his body. There had never been any question of how she would respond to him. Just because she knew that letting anything happen would be a bad idea didn't mean that she didn't want him, that she didn't want to forget all the reasons why she shouldn't do it, and just take what she wanted, to hell with the consequences.

But then her better judgment had caught up with her. How could she do her job tomorrow? How could she be convincingly in love with someone else, even if just for the cameras, if she allowed herself to think, to feel, how much she was in love with Ethan?

And what did he think he was doing, kissing her like that, like he had some sort of right to grab her and kiss her with no warning? She'd told him and told him that wasn't what she wanted. He was infuriating.

"Look, can we just go for dinner or something?" he said. "Talk properly?"

Abby could feel a plan forming. She couldn't have him thinking he could just walk in here, expecting her to go along with him.

"Sure. Saturday?"

Chapter Thirteen

"So, where are we heading?" Ethan asked as they climbed into the car. She'd asked him if she could take care of booking somewhere for dinner, seeing how she was local and knew the area.

"Oh, it's pretty special this place, you'll see," Abby said, smiling mischievously as she slid in behind the steering wheel.

She tried to keep her eyes on the road. Easier said than done when she had the image of Ethan waiting for her in the hotel lobby burned into her retinas. No one in real life looked like that, surely. She risked a little peek out of the corner of her eye, just to check that she wasn't making it up. Oh God. He just looked so… so…*good.*

He was looking smarter than she'd seen him since they'd been in the UK. He'd lived in jeans while they were on set, but now he was looking sharp. The suit had to be made to measure, nothing off the peg could look that good, and she'd had to force herself not to stare at his arse as he walked across the lobby. When he'd spotted her waiting behind him, he'd given her a smile, the lines around his eyes crinkling at the sight of her. He'd walked slowly up to her, and stopped just a few inches closer than she would have liked. With him that close, it was difficult to remember to breathe, never mind speak coherently. She'd dragged her eyes up his chest, to take in the lines of his face.

When her eyes had met his, his smile widened.

"You ready to go?"

She'd nodded, not trusting herself not to dribble if she opened her mouth to speak.

In rehearsals, around her colleagues, in front of the cameras, she could almost forget that he looked like this. She was spending a very large proportion of the day feeling someone else's emotions, after all: hers were easy to keep on a backburner. But away from location she no longer had someone else to hide behind, and now alone in a confined space with Ethan her own desires flooded back.

As the roads twisted and turned she could see Ethan swiping sideways glances at her every few minutes. It was funny how familiar the roads seemed. She hadn't even lived in the village for years before she left the UK, since she'd moved to London for drama school, but her body seemed to remember the roads perfectly, swinging the car into the corners as if she'd never been away.

Abby saw Ethan's shoulders drop slightly when she finally turned into the driveway. She'd put it off for as long as she could, but her mother would be furious if she found out Abby had been in the country and not visited. It was Ethan's fault that she was having to have dinner with her parents; she'd never have had to do this if she wasn't filming here, so the least he could do was act as moral support. Or a distraction.

With someone else there it was unlikely that her parents would take enough notice of her to really get stuck into her faults. Or ask too many questions about what she'd been doing. It probably would have been kinder to warn him about it in advance though.

"So…we're here?" Ethan asked.

Desperately hoping I'll say no, Abby thought.

"Yep, dinner with the Smiths, aren't you glad you asked me now?" After living with Ethan's subtle manipulations, Abby couldn't deny that she was pleased to get one up on him this time.

"Sure. Of course. I had something a little more…intimate…in mind, but it'll be nice to meet your parents."

Nice? How little he knew.

"You say that now…"

Abby drew in a deep breath and pulled her shoulders back as she rang the doorbell. She'd warned her mother that she'd be bringing a friend to dinner, but she hadn't told her who. Her mum didn't really follow the movie business, anyway; she considered it far beneath her, so she might not even know who Ethan was. Abby hoped that would be the case. Her mother would be an unbearable sycophant to his face if she knew; Ethan had enough money that even her mother could overlook a connection to the "entertainment" world. She wondered which would be the lesser of two evils, her mother fawning over him because she knew he was rich, or her being rude because she didn't.

"Abigail! Darling, do come in, and your friend of course. It's so lovely to see you, it's been *so* long." Of course accompanied by a pointed raise of the eyebrow. "Now, do introduce me to your friend."

"Mum, this is Ethan. Ethan, my mother, Rosemary Smith."

"Lovely to meet you Mrs. Smith." Ethan didn't miss a beat, ever the charmer. "You have a lovely home."

It seemed that Ethan's charm worked on her mother just as well as it did on everyone else—she gave a girlish giggle.

"Do call me Rosemary—Mrs. Smith sounds so…so old! Now, Abigail, why don't you take your friend through to meet your father, he's in the parlor reading the newspaper, and then you can come and help me in the kitchen."

Abby turned to walk down the hallway with Ethan, reeling slightly from her mother's disposition. Maybe the years had changed her mother as well as her. She hadn't said anything remotely disparaging; really, a slightly raised eyebrow was nothing compared to what she had been expecting. It was early days, but perhaps…

"Of course, it looks like you've spent plenty of time in the kitchen while you've been away. I thought these actress types were all skin and bones. You're looking…well, fat, darling." A tap on the bottom added injury to insult. It was said at barely more than a whisper, but the surprise on Ethan's face told Abby he had heard nonetheless.

Abby wished she didn't have to leave Ethan behind with her father. She hated to admit it to herself, but she really was hoping she could rely on him for support. Things hadn't been perfect between them in LA, but there had been a lot of good. Perhaps they could be friends, if nothing else. She certainly needed one of those tonight.

Her father barely looked up from the paper when they walked into the room.

"Dad, this is Ethan."

A grunt told her that he'd heard them.

"Nice to meet you, Mr. Smith. I believe we're compatriots?"

Ethan waited for a response, but Abby's dad just went back to his paper. Ethan looked across at Abby, hoping for assistance. It was cruel, but she couldn't help but enjoy Ethan's squirming. He'd called all the shots when she'd been staying at his place; now he was flailing. She heard her mother calling from the kitchen and shrugged at Ethan as he silently pleaded with her not to leave him.

She crossed the small hallway, noticing that the aspidistra still had pride of place on the sideboard, and a pen lay on top of the message pad on the telephone table. Everything just as she remembered.

"Come on, darling. I told you I needed your help, what have you been doing in there?"

Abby steeled herself. Now that she'd got her alone, she dreaded to think what her mother might say. "Sorry, I didn't want to just leave Ethan on his own—we've only just got here."

"Don't whine, darling. It's not attractive. You'll never get him to marry you if he hears you talking like that. You'll be forced down the whole 'happy accident' route if you're not careful. You're running out of time, you know."

Abby bit her tongue. So that's the direction this was going to go. She prepared herself for an evening's worth of questions about her plans for marriage. Perfect. Abby could only hope that her mother wouldn't be so obvious in front of Ethan.

At least she could be grateful that thirty years of living with her mother had reduced her father to a grunting, monosyllabic fool.

"So this friend of yours then."

Here we go…

"Yes. Ethan."

"How long have you been…courting?"

"Courting, Mum? No one's courted for fifty years."

"Well, whatever they call it then. How long have you been 'going out' with him? I assume you've already slept with him. Girls like you always do." Delivered through lips so pursed Abby marveled that sound could pass through them.

"I'm not 'going out' with him. I told you on the phone, he's a colleague and a friend."

"Really, well, you don't normally bring male friends home. You got your mother's hopes up. I thought you'd at least have some sort of *arrangement* to announce, even if you're not properly engaged. I didn't expect you to have done that well."

"It's not like that." Abby felt compelled to try and correct her mother, though she knew it would be impossible. "We're friends back home—"

"You *are* home." And didn't she know it. Her mother's irrational loathing for her career reared its head.

"We're friends in LA and he's been living in a hotel for months. I thought he might enjoy your cooking and some company, that's all."

Thankfully that seemed to shut her up for now; Abby knew that the shortcut to her mother's good side was always her cooking. Abby stirred the rich, shiny sauce simmering on the hob and wondered where the next barb would come from.

"So what exactly have you been up to *over there*? You never tell us anything about what you're doing. Of course the silence spoke volumes about your little 'career.'" Her mother could never actually bring herself to say the words Los Angeles, never mind Hollywood; it was far too vulgar in her opinion, and the word *career* brought out an actual snarl.

"Oh you know, this and that." Abby tried to keep her voice light—the last thing she wanted was for her mother to realize she was onto a fruitful line of enquiry. "I've just been working to pay the rent really until the right script came along."

"Let me guess, you've been waitressing at some greasy little café?" Abby suspected that her mother's insults wouldn't feel quite as sharp if they weren't so close to the truth.

"I have been, actually. It's been great." Okay, *great* was a stretch, but she wasn't going to admit that. "But I had to leave when I decided to take this part."

"Decided to take it, indeed. As if you were in a position to turn it down when you've been telling me you were just a waitress."

"Actually, Rosemary, she was pretty hard to convince."

Abby's face lit up at the sound of his voice—salvation. She smiled up at him. She couldn't fault his timing. At this moment, she couldn't work out what she was more grateful to him for—rescuing her career or rescuing her from her mother. It was a close call.

Looking at him lounging in the kitchen doorway, she was reminded of how she had felt the first time she had seen him. She had been so desperate to get him out of the diner, but not so desperate that she had been able to ignore the beautiful lines of his bone structure, the way his thick, dark hair fell forwards to frame chocolate-colored eyes. Back then, she'd had every reason to want him out of her life. And even that hadn't kept her away. She felt the heat of desire start to grow deep down in her stomach and knew that she was in trouble. Again.

What had she been thinking? Spending time with Ethan, away from work, was a seriously bad idea. It was going to get her heart broken. The full force of her feelings for him, which she'd been managing so well to ignore, was coming back to her.

She could feel the familiar pull towards him, and she worried that even knowing that he didn't love her wasn't going to be enough to keep her away. If he still wanted her in his bed, then how was she supposed to be able to resist? When she saw him looking like that, and remembered how good it had felt to be close to him…

She thought back to the last couple of days they had spent together at his house in LA—they had some seriously unfinished business. Maybe it would be easier to move on if things weren't so unfinished between them. The way Abby felt looking at him, she wanted their business *finished* as soon as possible. But that didn't mean it was a good idea. They were working together. And how was she ever meant to trust that he really wanted her after what had happened, or whether she just made good business sense to him?

Abby could hear her mother talking away to herself as she bustled around. Well, she must have thought that she was talking to Ethan, but he was walking across the kitchen towards her, his eyes fixed intently on her face. He leant his head close to hers when he reached her side, and whispered in her ear.

"Why are you blushing?"

"No reason."

Ethan simply raised an eyebrow and answered the question Rosemary had just asked him. Thank God he was still paying attention.

"Abby, don't just stand there looking useless. You take up far too much room for me to be expected to keep walking around you. Lay the table and call your father."

Abby's mother gave her a shrewd glance; maybe Ethan hadn't been so on the ball after all. Her mother seemed to go from acidic to sickly sweet in an instant, and Abby never knew which of the two she was going to get.

Ethan followed her into the dining room. Abby was tempted to pull the door shut behind them and press her face into Ethan's chest until he promised to drive her back to the hotel. But she was the one that had got them into this situation—God knows what she'd been thinking—so now she'd just have to man up and see it out.

She was reaching into the cabinet for wine glasses when she sensed Ethan standing close behind her; her body flushed with heat, just from standing so close to him. It would be so easy to fall back…

Ethan had obviously read her mind—a hand curved around her hip and pulled her back against him. She held her breath. Was she really going to do this? Allow herself to get close to him again?

No. She refused to allow herself to relax into his chest. But being so close to him, the anger and frustration that had been swirling through Abby's mind evaporated, leaving a quiet that she had never experienced while in the house with her mother.

They heard footsteps in the hallway. Abby folded the crochet table runner and placed it on the dresser, next to her mother's collection of porcelain figurines. Ethan took the glasses from her hands and started to set the table.

• • •

"Ethan, what do you do?"

Her father had barely spoken since they'd arrived, but he managed to pack maximum embarrassment into five words. Sure, these Hollywood types *said* they wanted a normal life, but Abby wondered when was the last time Ethan had met someone who didn't know what he did, who he was. He didn't seem to be offended, though. *Maybe he's enjoying the novelty of anonymity*, she thought to herself.

"I'm a film producer, sir." Abby recognized Ethan's most charming smile. She was flattered that he was bringing out the big guns to try and impress her father. It was sweet, really, that he was making such an effort.

Her father grunted in response. Hopefully that would be the last they heard from him.

"So, tell us about how you two met." Rosemary took over the role of Chief Embarrassment Officer. She was clearly just going to ignore what Abby had told her about them working together. Abby looked at Ethan in the seat beside her and tried to apologize to him with her eyes.

"Well, I saw Abby on TV when I was in the UK, and knew that I had to cast her in my movie. I managed to track her down at work and introduced myself."

"Oh, how perfectly lovely."

Abby rolled her eyes. Ethan was clearly working some sort of voodoo magic. Normally any mention of Abby's acting career was met with pursed lips and gravity-defying eyebrows. It seemed that, as ever, the normal rules didn't apply for Ethan Walker.

"Abigail, why don't you tell us what you've been up to since you left? You write so rarely we feel like we know nothing about your life anymore. When we didn't hear, we just assumed of course that your little experiment wasn't working out. Of course I could have told you before you left that you'd just end up with some crummy little job. And you could have had that here, you know. No need to travel at all." Apparently the Ethan effect had its limits.

"Oh, well, you know…" Abby tried to think of something to say that wouldn't immediately incite her parents' disapproval. "Sometimes it takes a while to get established, and then I wanted to be sure I chose the right project." A snort from her mother indicated that she didn't believe it for a second. Not entirely fair, Abby thought, it wasn't like it was a complete lie.

"And I couldn't believe my luck when she finally agreed to my movie. It took me long enough to convince her." Ethan to the rescue. Again.

"Ah, well, I heard the casting couch is how things work over there."

Abby choked on her potato gratin. *Oh. My. God. Did she really just say that?*

"I think you've got the wrong idea, Mrs. Smith." Abby recognized the warning tone in Ethan's voice—he was obviously furious but trying to contain it. "Abby and I are just friends and colleagues. And I can assure you, she was cast in this role entirely on merit. Your daughter is a wonderful actress."

And there it was, the "my daughter is an actress" face. Her mother looked as if she were sucking on a particularly unpleasant lemon. Laced with arsenic.

"Oh, I don't blame you. I know my daughter's very attractive. She gets that from me." *She's trying to flirt, even when accusing her daughter of sleeping around for financial gain? Unbelievable.* "And I suppose you just take it when it's offered. I can't imagine that she was very subtle, was she. She's always been very…shall we say… ambitious?"

She could see that Ethan was still furious on her behalf, but her parents would never guess. As ever, he was the perfect guest; only Abby would notice the clenched jaw and ice in his eyes.

Abby couldn't pretend his level of control.

She slammed her cutlery down on the table, pushed her chair back, and stood up. Her mother looked up, surprised. "Whatever's wrong, darling?"

"We're leaving. Ethan."

"Right behind you."

• • •

When they were safely in the car, Abby's knuckles turned white as she gripped the steering wheel. "I can't believe she said that. I'm so sorry, they're…they're just…awful."

"Abby, don't worry, you don't have to apologize. I just can't believe she would say something like that about you."

"It was a nightmare. I can't believe she would accuse you of something like that. That she would think I was capable of it too."

"Really, honey, it doesn't matter what she thinks of me. I'm just sorry she upset you."

"I can't believe I dragged you here to sit through that. I'm sorry, it was so selfish, but I couldn't face it on my own. It would have been a hundred times worse if you weren't there."

Ethan reached for her hand and Abby marveled at the intensity of feeling concentrated into that one small part of her body. His bruising kiss in her trailer had been intense, but this was different. This tiny touch was full of promise. If she wanted it to be. She pulled her hand away.

"It's okay. At least it's over now. And you have to admit that in time we'll probably think it was pretty funny. I don't think I've ever been accused of the casting couch before," Ethan said. "Not to my face, anyway."

"God, if she actually knew what had gone on—"

"But she doesn't. That's just between you and me and no one need ever know about it if that's what you want."

What she wanted was for him to suddenly realize he was in love with her and shout it from the rooftops. But given that that was never going to happen, that his seduction of her had just been a means to an end, keeping a lid on their liaison was probably a good idea.

"So, are you ready to drive, or do you want me to take over?"

"It's fine, I'll drive. I think I've calmed down enough to see straight now."

"Shall we stop for a drink on the way?"

"Actually, I think that maybe a drink would be good. After Mum, I need to cool down a bit."

Abby drove towards the pub in the village. She had escaped here after many a family meal before squaring her shoulders and heading home to face her mother. She wondered what Ethan would make of it. It wasn't the Hollywood version of an English country pub—all Farrow and Ball and ruddy-cheeked farmers—it was more of a sticky floor and meat raffle sort of place.

They walked into the pub and it seemed as if everyone in the building turned to look at them. *So much for keeping this just between us,* Abby thought. Abby had lived in this village her whole life, and the regulars at the Fox and Hound hadn't changed much in that time. No doubt her mother would get a full report of her behavior in the morning. She approached the bar with trepidation.

"If it isn't Abby Smith!" She smiled as she recognized Bill, the landlord. The years she had been away hadn't been terribly kind to him, but his good humor still sparkled in his eyes. "And with Hollywood in tow. Nice to meet you, Mr. Walker." He shook Ethan's hand across the bar. "We're all very proud of our Abby so we were very excited to read about your new project. And you're very welcome here."

Abby was overwhelmed by the warmth and affection in his voice. She'd not really been in here since she left home. But now she saw the pictures on the wall behind the bar. There were framed magazine articles from her TV days, and one of her receiving the best actress award at the British Soap Awards. She was genuinely touched by the gesture, glad to have her home village proud of what she'd achieved, even if her parents couldn't be.

"Ethan, this is Bill, he's been in charge of this place for as long as I can remember."

"Aye, I have, and I could tell you some stories if I were so inclined. New Year's Eve 2003 might be a good place to start, I believe..."

A look of horror crossed Abby's face. New Year's Eve 2003. She couldn't believe Bill remembered that. She'd been caught snogging some boy in the car park and then thrown up on his shoes. And on his shirt. And on Bill when he'd come to see if she was okay. Thinking about it, she was surprised that that story had never reached the magazines. She realized she owed Bill—big time. She'd forgotten just how many of her secrets he'd been privy to over the years.

She bought Ethan a pint of proper English ale, and a half for herself, and they found themselves a booth in a quiet corner.

"So that was quite something. Is your mother always like that?"

"Are you joking? That was best behavior—why do you think I wanted to take you home with me? I knew she'd hold back at bit if you were there; normally it's non-stop criticism from the minute I walk in the door."

"So I was just a human shield?" The smile in his eyes told her he wouldn't have minded if he was.

"No, it's not like that, I just thought you would charm her into better behavior, and it worked. At least to start with. I think the effect might have started to wear off a bit."

"And here I was thinking that you just wanted me to meet your parents. I thought maybe you were getting all serious on me."

She guessed that wouldn't have been welcome. Steamy kiss or not, Ethan was still not looking for a relationship, and Abby wasn't looking to get her heart broken.

"Ethan..."

"So, err, what were we saying?"

Abby laughed at his blatant attempt at levity. It hadn't worked.

"Oh, I think we were just generally cursing my mother."

"So normally she's worse than that? Has she always been this way?"

"To some degree. When I was a child it was easier. I would usually go along with what she wanted, so she had no cause to complain. It was only when I started to insist that I was serious about a career in acting that she became quite so venomous. I don't know why she was so against it, but she's always liked to keep up appearances, and a daughter who was an actress just wasn't really going to cut it with her. But I think what really killed her was the fact that I wouldn't take her word for what was best for me. Like I said, until that point, I'd just gone along with what she wanted, so my rebellion, as she saw it, was completely out of the blue. I'd changed into a different person. The truth was, until that point there had been nothing in my life worth rocking the boat for. But I knew I had to fight for this."

"Wow, remind me not to cross you."

"I think we might be a little late for that. But I'm glad we're talking again."

"Me too. I've missed you, you know."

Her eyes widened in surprise. No, she didn't know.

"I hated that I had to leave LA so soon," he continued, "but things needed doing over here that only I could see to. I thought about flying back to see you, even if only for a few hours, but I wasn't sure that was what you wanted."

"It wasn't," she confessed. "I was still angry. But I know now—" she took a deep breath, "—that although what you did really hurt, you hadn't meant it to. I needed a bit of space and perspective…"

"And now?"

"I'm happy we can be friends again."

Chapter Fourteen

Abby couldn't believe how the last few months had changed her life. It was as if everything she had ever dreamed of had come true. She was shooting the last day on the most incredible film. She loved waking up in the morning knowing that she was going to spend the day exploring her character, and she was learning more about her craft all the time. Her drama school training and the experience from her soap opera apprenticeship had soon come back to her, and she could tell from watching the faces of those around her that she hadn't lost her skills.

The weight of expectation from every one of the cast and crew, who knew how much faith was being placed in her, had been heavy on her shoulders. And to start with naturalism and spontaneity had been almost impossible. But as she'd improved, she saw trust and faith in her start to grow. It had been a long time since Abby had made new friends, and she reveled in her newfound freedom to hold a conversation without dread of exposure and shame.

After two years of near-complete isolation, the intimacy of sharing her life and her space with so many people was intoxicating.

And then there was Ethan.

Since that night at her parents', they'd fallen into a friendship, and after the swift, chaste kiss on the cheek she'd given him when he walked her to her room, Ethan seemed to have got the message that that was all she was prepared to offer. They hadn't had much time alone together anyway. Both of their schedules were pushed to the limit trying to fit in all of the scheduled shooting, and Abby had come onto the project so late that there were a million other things to do as well: last minute wardrobe fittings, press commitments, meet and greets with key investors.

It was better to keep him at a safe distance. That's what she told herself over and over, every time that Ethan looked over at her and her heart started beating faster as she remembered what it was like to kiss him, to be kissed by him, to run her hands over his chest and down his belly. But what would be the point of kissing him now? What would be the point of opening up to him, showing him how she felt, and then being left broken when he decided that he'd had enough? That he'd had his run of good publicity out of her and now wanted something—someone—different.

But she couldn't tell him that, not without him seeing how she felt. And the only thing worse than being in love with Ethan Walker would be him knowing, and not loving her back.

• • •

She looked so cute, sitting there in a dressing gown over her clothes, trying to keep warm. And failing miserably, judging by the blue tinge of her lips. She could have gone back to her trailer, should have gone back, but he knew her, and knew that she wouldn't feel right to do that when the rest of the cast and the extras were shivering in the marquee. She had been the same for the whole shoot, and he supposed he couldn't expect her to be any different just because it was the last day of filming. He fetched two cups of tea from the urn, walked over to where she was sitting, and pulled up a plastic picnic seat. He pressed a hot cup of tea into her hands and felt the heat pass from his fingers to hers as he let his hand linger, trying to prolong the contact.

"Not much longer now," he promised. "We nearly had it on that last take. One more and then we can get you into the warm."

She smiled at him. "It's fine. I know these things take time."

"It's not fine," he told her. Anytime he saw her like this, looking less than contented with the world, he just wanted to take away whatever it was that was making her sad, angry, or—in this case—cold.

He knew that she was still holding back on him. He was happy that they were talking again, but she was still so careful around him. So guarded. There had to be something else. He just wanted to know what it was, why she was still holding him at a distance. If he could just get through to her…

"Are you looking forward to tonight?" The cast and crew—well, the ones who weren't being bussed straight to Heathrow the minute the cameras stopped rolling—were planning a bit of a wrap party, ahead of the glitzy official Hollywood one they'd be going to in a few days.

"I guess," Abby replied. "I can't believe it's here already."

"Your first movie shoot finished. How does it feel?"

Her brows drew together in concentration as she considered her answer. "I'd say, at the moment, it feels…cold. Kinda numb."

He laughed. "Can I get you anything? More tea?"

She gave him a shrewd look that he was pretty sure he didn't deserve. "I'm fine, thanks."

"Right, and do you usually look blue when you're fine?" He reached for her hand and showed her her fingernails, looking decidedly grey under the clear polish.

She snatched her hand back.

"Ethan, don't."

"What? It was perfectly innocent. I was just demonstrating to you that you are seriously cold. If you weren't so stubborn and—"

"I'm stubborn? You're the one who won't let this drop. I thought we were past this."

"Past what?" Ethan asked, feigning ignorance. "You've lost me this time."

"Oh, you know exactly what I mean. The strokey finger thing just now. I've told you before, Ethan, that's not what I want."

Except he was pretty sure that she did.

"Why not?" If she was going to be evasive, perhaps the only way to counter it was being brutally direct.

"Well, because…because we work together for a start."

He checked his watch. "Right, for another two hours or so."

She sighed. "It's not just that. You know it's not. What about everything that happened before?" Finally he was getting somewhere. Maybe if she would just open up to him, they could actually see where this thing could go. Because if there was one thing he knew, it was that ignoring it was not making it go away. Surely she could see that as clearly as he could.

"I made a mistake, Abby. I'm sorry, I really am. But I don't think that's it. You said yourself that you'd forgiven me…" *Please God, don't take that back now.*

"It's not that." She stilled, and he saw that look come back. The one he'd seen so many times at his house in LA without truly knowing what it meant. She was risk assessing. Weighing up every word—what she could say, what she couldn't. The cost of every syllable. She was still hiding. Not from the world anymore, but from him.

• • •

Abby took a deep breath as she walked into the hotel bar. It had taken a long soak in a hot bath to get the feeling back into the ends of her toes, and they weren't thanking her now for being crammed into high heels. But she felt like she needed armor, and in the absence of Kevlar, the mysterious confidence that seemed to come from a decent pair of stilettos would have to do. Ethan would still tower over her, of course, an extra three inches wasn't going to change that, but it was all she could muster at short notice.

The first thing she saw when she walked into the room was Ethan's arse, firm and tight and clad in expensive-looking denim as he leant nonchalantly against the bar. He was so doing this on purpose. The fake double take when he looked over his shoulder and saw her standing in the doorway confirmed what she suspected. Mirror behind the bar: he'd seen her coming.

She walked over to him slowly, realizing after a couple of strides that the shoes were a mistake. From the way that Ethan's eyes widened as they travelled from shoe, to ankle, to hip, and back again, the extra couple of inches in confidence were somewhat outweighed by the fact that Ethan seemed to like them. A lot. Up in her room, where she'd had to practice walking in the shoes—after two years in flats her calf muscles had not been happy—the sway of her hips, the way they tipped her forwards, hadn't seemed quite so…provocative. She reached the bar and leant back against it, trying to relieve the pressure on her toes. Ethan's eyes met hers, and then dropped down to the silky black top she'd decided on—high cowl neck, very modest—over the skinny jeans to the stilettos she'd had to borrow from wardrobe.

"Nice shoes."

He could bloody well stop smirking.

"Killing me already," she bit back, slipping them off and stepping barefoot onto the floor of the bar. She looked up at Ethan's face, and then down to her eye line, right across the broadest part of his chest. She really could do with those extra few inches, but as always with Ethan, the cost was just too high.

He handed her a glass of red wine.

"Did I guess right?"

"Do I have a choice?"

"You always have a choice." She took the glass from him and tried to convince herself that he was just talking about the drink.

"Right…thanks." She waited for Ethan to start with the small talk, anything to break the awkward silence that was developing. She didn't trust herself to open her mouth without blurting out something stupid, something that would start a fight, or something more dangerous.

She was rescued by Matt, who walked up to the bar and grinned at her.

"Abby! You look great. Are you two coming to sit with the rest of us?" From the corner of her eye she could see Ethan's scowl, and knew instantly that he didn't want her to go.

"Of course! Lead the way." Abby grabbed her shoes and walked over with him, but Ethan remained standing at the bar. When she looked back at him, he seemed to be just as transfixed by her legs as he had been before. Shit. Maybe it was the jeans.

Abby sat drinking her wine, enjoying listening to the hum of conversation around her. She sank further into the cushions of the chair, and laughed at the sight of some of her colleagues dancing. The evening seemed to have a strange end-of-term disco feel about it, and the strictures and constraints of the work-intensive weeks were being well and truly worked off on the dance floor. The lights in the bar dropped a little more until it could genuinely be considered mood lighting, and the live band started playing in the corner of the room.

"Come on, we're all dancing, no excuses now," Molly said to her, grabbing her hands and pulling her to her feet.

"But my shoes—" Abby started to protest. She'd not been able to bring herself to cram her aching toes back into them.

"Will be waiting for you when you get back," Molly insisted, dragging Abby behind her.

Gradually, Abby let her body relax into the rhythm of the music, lifting her arms and moving her hips in time, remembering how much she used to enjoy this. Before. When she had friends and boyfriends to go dancing with. When Matt came to dance beside her, she thought nothing of it. The whole team was dancing together in a slightly sweaty, very uncoordinated, somewhat tipsy mass.

That was, until the music slowed, and Matt grabbed her hand and slid a friendly arm around her waist. Abby could see over

Matt's shoulder that plenty of other people were dancing in the same way; relaxing into the hold, she shuffled around to the music. She laughed as Matt lifted his arm and twirled her underneath; then brought her back close and dipped her backwards. But from her inverted position she saw something that was certain to ruin their fun—a pair of familiar thighs striding towards her.

Ethan arrived as her head returned to its usual upright position, and the blood swam in her ears slightly as she tried to focus.

"I think I'll be…" Matt beat a hasty retreat, not even bothering to finish his sentence under the fire of Ethan's stare.

"What now, Ethan?" Abby asked as his arm replaced Matt's around her waist, his touch more possessive than friendly.

"I'm rescuing you. Thought you'd be grateful, actually."

"Rescuing me?" She sighed, exasperated. "Why on earth would I need rescuing?"

"Because Matt had his hands all over you, that's why. You told me you didn't feel that way about him; I didn't think his pawing would be welcome."

"Oh, come on. That wasn't pawing, that was dancing—"

"Slow dancing," Ethan corrected.

"It was dancing slowly," Abby insisted, trying to pull away from him. "You're jealous, aren't you? Are we really going to go through this again?"

"I am not jealous," Ethan growled, pulling the arm around her waist even tighter.

Well how else was she supposed to explain what had just happened? She'd been perfectly happy. She hadn't done anything that would make Ethan feel like she needed rescuing, and yet he'd felt the need to barge in and interrupt.

"I thought I was doing you a favor. Remind me not to bother next time. But don't tell me you're not glad that I did it."

"I told you I was fine before."

"Oh, I'm not talking about before," he said, his voice dropping, becoming more intimate. "I'm talking about now. Tell me you're not enjoying this." She tried to move away from the fingers tracing tiny circles at her waist, but to no avail. The arm remained clamped around her, preventing her from moving her body even a millimeter away from Ethan's. And as much as she tried, she couldn't ignore how good this felt, how right it was to be back in his arms.

Ethan must have sensed her agreement, must have felt her relax fractionally into him, because the arm round her back became more embracing than confining, his hand started to move round to the small of her back, stroking slowly up and down her spine. He drew their hands close into his chest.

"Ethan, people are going to talk." This couldn't be more different to how she'd been dancing with Matt. If you could even call this dancing. Ethan was still holding her so tight that they didn't actually seem to be moving too much.

"I don't care," he murmured. "Do you?"

For the first time, Abby's conscience didn't automatically scream *yes*. People might talk. She'd probably rather that they didn't, but did she care enough to stop this? To move away? What's the worst that they could say now? That she'd been having an affair with the boss? Maybe they would. Maybe the old casting couch rumors would be circulating again. But for the first time in years, Abby realized she didn't care. She'd proven to everyone on the movie that she had won that job on merit. They couldn't deny that now. And if they did, they were just malicious gossips. And why should she give this up—this feeling—just to appease them.

She rested her head on Ethan's shoulder. "No. Let them talk."

Ethan's hand crept further up her back to play with the ends of her hair and his chin came down to rest on the top of her head.

"I'd forgotten—" she started, before stopping herself. She hadn't forgotten—she just hadn't allowed herself to remember.

"What?" Ethan asked, but Abby shook her head. "How well we fit?" He tucked her body even closer to his. Abby's eyes widened. How could he know what she was thinking? When he dropped a kiss on the top of her head she stopped trying to figure it out. Decided to just enjoy these sensations, the feeling of being in his arms again. The whole evening had a surreal feel to it. A wrap party with half the cast missing. Her last night at home before flying…home. Being with Ethan, knowing that she could never *be* with him.

She reminded herself for the thousandth time of all the reasons she couldn't be with him. He didn't do serious. It wasn't what he wanted. She would always be business to him. It would never last. These were all very good reasons not to enter into a relationship with him. But for all her reasoning, she couldn't seem to summon up one reason why she couldn't have him *tonight.*

Could she really just spend one night with him? And then head back to LA tomorrow as if nothing had happened? She had no doubt that it would hurt. But doing nothing hurt too. And how much worse would it be after a month, a year, a decade of wondering what might have been?

Ethan's hand started to drift dangerously southwards, too far south for a public place—definitely too far south for a public place when they were surrounded by their colleagues—and she knew that she could. Knew that she had to. She tilted her head up to look at Ethan, the action pressing her hips forward against him, and a blush spread up her face as she felt his reaction.

Ethan's eyes darkened as he took in the desire written plainly on her face.

"I was thinking—"

"—let's go."

He dropped the arm from behind her back and kept her in front of him as they walked out the bar, his fingers gripping her hip tight. Abby kept her head determinedly forwards. Better not to know if anyone saw, she thought to herself. She briefly considered going back for her shoes, but thought better of it. She was pretty sure that whatever Ethan had in store for her, it was worth a pair of stilettos.

The elevator ride was agony. Ethan hadn't let her go, and she was afraid that if she spoke, if she moved, that she would break the spell. Was this really going to happen? They'd been so close to this before. He pulled her tighter against him and she held her breath, overwhelmed by the feel of his hard, muscular frame wrapped around her, unable to think as his lips teased her neck and whispered in her ear.

At the door to Abby's suite, she stopped. Could she really do this? Just one night? One night stands were not really her style. But what was worse—a lifetime of not knowing what it would be like to make love to Ethan—the only man she had ever loved? A three-week affair, with him gradually losing interest, until he decided to move on to someone else? Or leaving this room tomorrow, satisfied and sated, but knowing that it could never happen again. Satisfied and sated it was. She just had to remember that this wasn't really real. He wasn't hers to keep. She couldn't let herself forget that.

She opened the door and Ethan's lips were on hers before it had closed behind him.

Her hands were grabbing at his shirt and T-shirt, pulling them over his head, when a groan escaped her lips. It was so good to be kissing him; she still couldn't quite believe he was here. For tonight at least. If she wanted to she could just…her hand found its way around his hips and stoked the firm curve of his arse. Delicious.

Ethan let out a growl, gripped her hard round the waist, and carried her to the bedroom.

And then somehow her own shirt was on the floor, she hadn't even had time to be nervous about it, and at last she had his skin against hers.

Chapter Fifteen

Abby woke with a ray of sunlight across one cheek and Ethan's chest pressed against the other. Her arm lay across his perfect stomach and she lifted it slightly, not wanting to wake him. It didn't work. The arm around her waist, which she hadn't noticed until just now, pinned her hard against him. There would be no escape. But she needed out. Nature called, and she had no intention of saying good morning with un-brushed teeth.

She was nervous, more so than she had been last night. What now? She had given in to her attraction, knowing that ending up in Ethan's bed was inevitable, whatever the consequences for her heart. But this wouldn't—couldn't—last. She would be on a plane today, and it would be over. Ethan didn't do serious—so neither could she.

She tried again to wriggle from underneath the arm pinning her against his side, resorting to prizing it away from her. So much for getting away without waking him. She suddenly found herself flipped over and pinned beneath his body, the weight of him pressing against her chest.

"And where do you think you're going?" he said, his voice husky.

"Um, bathroom?" Abby squeaked.

"Not yet you're not. Kiss me."

She turned her head, not wanting to risk morning breath.

"Now."

She forced her lips together, desperately trying not to think about waterfalls or running taps.

"*Now.*"

Well it was embarrassment by morning breath, or by something much worse. She picked the lesser of two evils and kissed Ethan back, opening her mouth to him. As a hand went to gently cup her breast, Abby saw her escape route. She pushed her hands against Ethan's chest and rolled out from underneath him. She managed to dodge the arm that tried to pull her back and walked to the bathroom, wishing halfway there that she were wearing a little more than nothing. Though when she turned back and saw the way Ethan was watching her, she thought maybe it wasn't so bad.

She pulled a comb through her hair, thankful that they didn't have an early start this morning. It had been an intense few weeks with early calls or night shoots almost every day. And now it would be back to LA and real life.

But Abby had been prepared to take a lifetime of missing Ethan for one glorious night in his bed. And glorious it had been—there was no doubt about that.

When she walked out of the bathroom, Ethan was still lying in the bed, his head propped up on one hand. He watched her walk across the room, and from the expression on his face, she guessed that he wasn't pleased with the addition of an enormous fluffy bathrobe.

"Morning." She smiled at him, her nerves returning a little.

Abby hesitated by the bed. Did she get back in? Did she suggest that they get up?

Ethan saved her from her pondering by reaching for the belt of her robe and pulling her down onto the bed.

"I hope you weren't thinking of going anywhere," he said between kisses. "I happen to know that you don't have to go to work today, and I need you back in here with me." Abby shrugged the robe off and climbed back into bed. Ethan kissed her again and all thoughts of leaving were wiped from her mind.

Much, *much* later Abby managed to rouse herself enough to look at the clock on the bedside table. Her car to the airport would be here in an hour and she still had to finish packing.

She was determined to walk away with dignity. She was going to get back to LA, unpack her suitcase, and concentrate on her career. Walking away from Ethan would be hard, but it was the right thing to do. It would only hurt more if she were to wait until he tired of her.

Ethan stirred in the bed. When his eyes opened, it took him a second to focus on her, and her full suitcase, and figure out what was going on.

"Going somewhere?" he asked sleepily.

"Yes, LA," she replied sharply. "As are you." *It's not fair to be mad at him*, she told herself. *You knew all along that this was what was going to happen, as did he. Play nice.* "I'm sorry. I think I'm just a bit tired. My car's going to be here in forty-five minutes."

"Forty-five minutes?" Ethan raised an eyebrow. Abby noticed the increasingly disturbed sheets and read his mind.

"Why, can you think of something we can do to pass the time?" If she had less than an hour left with him, it would be a crime to spend it doing anything else, she told herself, kicking off her shoes and reaching for the zip of her dress.

Chapter Sixteen

Ethan watched Abby from across the party. She'd been standing with that man for more than ten minutes, looking over her shoulder every thirty seconds or so. Why hadn't he got the message—she wasn't interested in him. She looked incredible, he admitted to himself. Her body was wrapped in bright blue silk, the color making her eyes pop out at him from across the room. Her hair shone, and smooth curls cascaded over her shoulder. But she looked nothing like as good as the last time he'd seen her, her hair a mess and her makeup smudged, sleeping in the crook of his arm.

He'd fallen asleep like that, but when he'd woken, she was gone. No note, nothing. He'd tried calling her before his flight, and again when he got back to LA, but she hadn't answered. Eventually he realized that she wasn't going to. If he wanted to talk to her, it was going to have to be face to face. Only he didn't know where she was staying. She'd given up that flea-pit of an apartment before she'd left for England, and his best guess was that she was holed up in a hotel somewhere until she got a new place sorted. Of course he could call in a few favors and find out where she was staying. It would be easy—take twenty minutes, tops.

But as she'd been ignoring him already, he didn't think that stalking would get himself back in her good books. He just wished he'd known what he'd done wrong. So he'd waited. The wrap party had been scheduled for five days after they got back, enough time to sleep off the worst of the jet lag, and so he'd decided that this would have to be it. They would have it out here, once and for all, and Abby would tell him why, after all they had been through together, she was still running. Still hiding.

She looked over her shoulder again, and this time she saw him.

The man she was speaking to must have seen the change in her face because he quickly took the hint and excused himself.

Their eyes met across the room, but he didn't see what he wanted in her eyes, he didn't see her wanting him, didn't see the lust that had been there that last night in England. He saw fear, again. He knew her well enough to know that that look meant her heart was racing and sweat was beginning to prickle on her forehead. Fight or flight was starting to kick in, and he knew which one was going to win out. She turned for the stairs.

He followed her up, and as he turned the corner, he saw her slip into one of the dressing rooms that had been set up to cater for the primping and preening of the flock of actresses who would be attending. When he tried the door, it was locked.

"Abby, are you in there?"

No response.

"Abby, I saw you come in here. I just want to know that you're okay." That wasn't all he wanted, but it was a start.

"I'm okay," she said through the door. He heard her take a deep, long breath, and then turn the lock.

"I'm fine, really," she said as she opened the door wide and stood in front of him, shoulders squared. "I just needed a quiet moment, it's so…intense out there…"

"I think we need to talk." He saw a moment's hesitation—as she considered pushing past him and running down the stairs, no doubt—but she stood aside, her body language inviting him into the room.

"What about, Ethan?"

He grabbed her hand and led her away from the door, over to a red velvet couch, plush and inviting in the glow from the gilt light fixtures.

"Well, for a start, we can talk about your little disappearing act," he said, sitting down and tugging on her hand until she sat beside him. "You know, the one where we spend the night together, and then you jump on a plane, give up the lease on your apartment, and stop answering your phone?"

Abby shifted uncomfortably in her seat. "Oh, come on, we both know what that night was. It was *one* night. I thought a clean break would be best."

He could actually see the front—see that she was forcing herself to say these words. That it wasn't what she really wanted.

"And what about what I wanted? What if I wanted more than one night, more than a fling? What if I wanted…more?" He didn't know where the words came from, but as soon as they left his mouth, he knew that they were true. With Abby, he would always want more. "It was just easier to run and hide, wasn't it? Like it was tonight."

"No—" He could see a slight tremble in her bottom lip. He wanted to stop pushing. Wanted to take her in his arms. But he had to know what it was she was so frightened of. Why she was so scared of letting him close.

He moved closer. The light from dozens of bulbs surrounding the mirror above the dresser was reflected in the perfect curls that fell over her shoulder. She looked beautiful. The perfect Hollywood princess. But he didn't want a Hollywood princess, he wanted Abby, and he wanted her looking the way he remembered every time he thought of her. He hated the public face that she was wearing tonight, the way that the stylists had tweaked and refined and perfected until she looked immaculate.

He wasn't even thinking as his fingers pulled through her hair. He just knew that he wanted her close. Wanted her. "I think I like this better when it's a little mussed up," he murmured. Her eyes widened, but she made no move to stop him. After he had ensured that every single ringlet had been teased, tangled, and messed out of place, he finally met her eyes.

His arm slid around her waist, drawing her close.

"Ethan, this isn't a good idea…"

Of course it wasn't a good idea. But it didn't matter. He had spent days thinking about this, thinking about having her in his arms again. This time the longing had been even more intense, now he knew what it was like to make love to her. With the hand that was still locked in her hair, he turned her face up to him, leaned forwards, and planted the gentlest of kisses on her lips.

I should not be doing this, Ethan told himself. He wanted to talk to her. Find out what had made her run. Tell her that whatever it was, he would sort it out. They could sort it out together. He had never felt this way before. This need to protect someone; the complete inability to stay away. With all the dozens of beautiful young women he'd dated over the years, he'd felt nothing but a mild interest. Lust, of course—and often. Determination, occasionally, and the excitement of the chase when someone played hard to get, thinking it would tie him down. But nothing like the last few days. The endless hours thinking about her, reliving their night together, trying to work out what had gone wrong. He didn't know what was happening to him; all he knew was that he needed her.

He watched her face and saw the confusion in her eyes. He hated that he was responsible for that confusion; for the fact that she doubted him. It was his fault. He had known the first minute he set eyes on this woman, months before they'd met, that she was different, that the way he felt about her was different. If he'd just been brave enough to admit it then, he wouldn't be looking at the distrust on her face. He couldn't tell her how he felt when he didn't understand it himself. But if he couldn't tell her, perhaps he could show her.

He kissed her, gently, tenderly, trying to show her how much she meant to him. Having her back in his arms, it felt like the past few days hadn't happened; now that they were together again it was as if they had never been apart. His body remembered every curve of hers and as she leaned into him and her hand reached up to pull his face closer he groaned, a thousand memories of their bodies pressed together just like this flooding back to him.

The kiss had started as a way to show her how he felt about her—he didn't know whether it was working, but the capacity for rational thought was rapidly deserting him. Just as he was starting to think that it might be, that Abby might be starting to understand how he felt, his cell phone started to ring. He swore under his breath, reached into his jacket pocket, and rejected the call. When he placed a hand on Abby's cheek, she looked at him, surprised.

"That could be important."

"I don't care. This is important."

He saw her eye the door. She was going to run again, he was sure of it.

Whatever he felt for her, whatever she might feel for him, it was never going to mean anything if she couldn't talk to him. If there was always going to be something standing between them. But he couldn't push her. If she didn't do this of her own volition, it would mean nothing.

• • •

Abby's eyes flicked between Ethan and the door. She should go. She should walk out of here and not look back, because staying could only mean one thing. She would tell him everything; she would lay all her secrets bare, and just have to hope he didn't run from her. Everything that she had been sure of was shifting beneath her feet. Ethan wasn't meant to chase her once he'd got what he wanted. He wasn't meant to be here, trying to persuade her that this wasn't just a fling. If he wanted to be with her, to try and make a relationship work, she would have to tell him everything. The sinking feeling in her gut confirmed to her what she already knew deep down. She wasn't avoiding a relationship with

Ethan because she was worried about his feelings—she was worried about hers.

She shouldn't, couldn't expect honesty from Ethan if she wasn't prepared to be open with him. But her secrets had kept her safe. After her attack, controlling who knew about it was the only protection she had left. A relationship with Ethan meant no more hiding. It meant everything out in the open.

She looked at him and saw the concern plain on his face. He didn't want to hurt her. If she was sure of nothing else she was sure that, in spite of their misunderstandings, Ethan wanted to protect her.

"Ethan, you don't understand. There are things…things that I haven't told you. I haven't told anyone…and I don't know if I can."

"And until you do, we can never know what this thing between us really is. Are you at least going to give it a chance?"

She slumped back and took a deep breath.

"The photos…" she started, not knowing how to put what had happened into words, how to make Ethan understand what had been taken from her. How exposed she had been. Ethan sat beside her on the couch, not saying a word, just taking her hand and holding it firmly in his own.

"I didn't mean … I didn't want…"

She realized that she wasn't making any sense. She would have to start at the beginning.

She told him of arriving for an audition, being given a cup of very strong, very bitter coffee, and she told him of waking up on a couch, hours later, facing a video camera, with just a few strange, hazy memories that could have been a dream. She told him that the only thing that really stuck in her mind was the painting above the couch. A huge, abstract thing with waves of bold color.

"I was scared. I just wanted to get out of there. I couldn't even put my finger on why. It wasn't until I got home and changed that

I realized my underwear was inside out. It hadn't been when I left the house that morning."

"The police..." Ethan started, wondering about the obvious question.

"I went to the police station. I was sure that they hadn't assaulted me physically, but whatever had happened wasn't good. In the waiting room I flicked through an old magazine, and that's when I saw her. An Aussie soap actress I'd met occasionally before she'd gone out to LA. Her career was really taking off, there was talk of the lead in the next James Cameron extravaganza, a L'Oreal campaign, and then 'intimate'—read nude and highly graphic—photos of her appeared and her career collapsed. And I knew absolutely that the same would happen to me, because there, just in the corner of the photo, was the painting that I remembered from earlier that day.

"I know that I should have reported what they did to me. If it happened now, I'm not sure that I'd make the same decision. But back then, all I could think was that telling anyone what had happened would mean the photos would definitely come out. That's what they wanted. To publish the photos, expose me, humiliate me. And that would be just as bad as them taking them in the first place. I know that the police and the courts and the law would protect me, but who's to say it would work? That someone wouldn't leak them online. No amount of legal action could undo that."

"So you hid."

"What choice did I have? Keeping this secret, it's been there, a physical thing, between me and everyone I've met since it happened. I know that keeping a part of myself back stops them getting too close, stops me getting hurt. Now you know every sordid little detail of my life, what's left to protect me?"

• • •

He took a deep breath, tried to compose himself.

"I love you."

"What did you say?" Abby asked, incredulous.

"I love you. That's what's going to stop you getting hurt." It was true. He knew it the moment she had told him what had really happened, what she had been through. He knew in that second that he would do anything in his power to stop her getting hurt like that again, because he loved her.

His phone rang again, this time he turned it off and flung it on the dressing table.

"But I thought…"

"I know what you thought. It was what I thought too. I thought that night would stop this feeling. This feeling that I can't get enough of you, but hot and frantic didn't satisfy. Slow and intense didn't work either. Whatever I do, whatever *you* do, I just want more. I'll always want more from you. I think I've loved you for weeks, months. Longer. I thought that maybe you felt the same way, but if I've made a mistake…" He started to pull his hand away, but she kept a firm hold on it.

"I do. I do feel the same way," she said quietly, looking up at him through her eyelashes.

"You love me?"

She gripped his hand harder and pulled herself across the space between them. "Of course I love you." But even as the euphoria bloomed across her face, a shadow of doubt chased after it.

"What is it?" he asked.

"Nothing, it's nothing." But it wasn't nothing, he could see that much. If she didn't tell him now, if she was still going to run from him … When she started speaking again he breathed a sigh of relief. "Actually, no, it's not nothing. I love you, and I want to be with you. Properly. But I know that you've never wanted a serious relationship. If that isn't what you want, I don't know that I can do this…"

He stared at her for a second, not quite believing that she hadn't understood him. How could she not see how much he wanted her, how much he loved her and needed her in his life? Forever.

"Abby, are you kidding? I never want to be away from you again. Ever. You know that you're going to marry me, right?"

She laughed gently. Okay, so maybe his delivery had lacked finesse. But he couldn't help it—she made him crazy.

"Says who?" she said.

"What?"

"Who says I'm marrying you?"

"What…" His heart fell. "You don't want to?"

"Not until you ask me properly."

He smiled again as he dropped to one knee without letting go of Abby's hand. "Abigail Smith, Abby Richards, my Abby, would you do me the very great honor of agreeing to be my wife?"

Abby said nothing for several seconds, but a smile spread from her lips to her eyes until her whole body was glowing with it.

"Of course I will." Her face broke out into an enormous grin as she pulled him up from the floor and wrapped her arms around him, tilting her head up for a kiss.

About the Author

Ellie Darkins is a writer and editor living in Warwickshire, England. When she's not tapping away at her keyboard she can usually be found next to the kettle, or in her local library sampling the coffee, cake, and romance novels.

A Sneak Peek from Crimson Romance
(From *Secretly* by Debra Kayn)

The gravel road crunched under the soles of Angie Swanson's Nike runners. The fierce wind blew off the mountain range and swept her honey-brown hair behind her shoulders. She stopped in the middle of Main Street and squinted into the setting sun, gazing down a barren, straight road.

Of all the places she never imagined herself ending up, it was Deadhorse, Oregon. Worse yet, she always dreamed she'd be working at a major spa, specializing in Swedish massage. Instead, she was the super pumper at her older brother Drew's gas station.

It was, in fact, The Gas Station. Drew couldn't even come up with a better name on the sign, despite her suggestions to glam it up into something more. Angie's Pumps, Octane in Lavender, or even leaning in the direction of hilarity with *Let us pump you up* would've been better than The Gas Station. Drew had rejected all of them for the nondescript, boring name; but that wasn't surprising. He lived in Deadhorse.

Dead. Horse.

She didn't belong here. The slow pace where people only talked about the weather and June Murphy's prized rose bushes outside the post office bored her to tears. To her, they were flowers. Red ones, that looked like any other rose bush in a million other front yards.

She had been born to do something big. Bigger than pumping gas in a deceased animal town where only the wind kept her company.

After spending four years at Washington State University, majoring in Journalism, she'd quickly learned after taking a community class on therapeutic massages that she wanted to change professions. So, she'd left her gopher position at the *Seattle Times*, and succeeded in landing a posh job at Le Massage. Then, three months ago, after working there almost two years, the spa closed. Unable to afford to keep renting the apartment she shared with her best friend, Jules, she'd taken up Drew's offer to work for him.

Temporarily, of course.

Every day, each longer and more depressing than the last, passed in a blur of mundane information overload, high-strung emotions, and the foolish realization that she should have bought stock in Doritos—for how much they were the main staple of her diet lately. Not to mention last week her father had dropped off her four-year-old half-sister and five-year-old half-brother for two days of fun with big sis while he vacationed with her stepmom. The past three months had been a painful lesson about living in Loserville.

She had to find a job before she lost the rest of her sanity. She glanced down at her sneakers and groaned. Seriously, what kind of place had cow shit in the middle of the road? Obviously there were some animals alive and kicking still around.

She dragged her foot behind her for ten paces, rechecked her sole, and declared it as clean as it'd get. Not that anyone would notice. The smell of gasoline on her clothes overrode *eau de toilette* poo.

Angie would give anything to escape and go back to Seattle. She sighed, gazing up into the sky. Whether it was because she'd hit rock bottom or simply because she wanted something better in her life than living her brother's dream, she'd started scouring the internet and applying for any job she qualified for. And still nobody hired her.

Something had to change soon. She sniffed, and raised her chin. The desire to ride the monorail and go shopping downtown at Nordstrom tempted her each day. But Seattle was twelve hours away. The price of gas alone was too much for her to rent a car to return to the Rose City to visit.

But until circumstances changed, she'd spend her free time pumping gas, washing windshields, and checking tire pressure. She hooked her thumbs in the front pockets of her shorts and walked back toward the gas station, which she'd closed an hour ago. With her brother gone to pick up another project car, she had to work alone. At least he was due back tomorrow, and she'd have someone to talk with during the day.

Distracted by the many things on her wish list, she gave the man leaning against the gas pump a cursory glance and opened her mouth to tell him the gas station was closed when recognition dawned on her. She gasped and covered her mouth.

Tall with huge shoulders, Gary Satchel, the Seattle Seahawks' wide receiver, hijacked her attention. She stood without saying a word, not believing he was here. But it was him. Not just anybody could pull off his size.

His well-worn Levi's, blue and silver Seattle Seahawks football jersey, six foot four inches tall with dark stormy eyes, the two inch scar running the length of his left cheekbone on his handsome face told her everything she needed to know. She raised her gaze and shouted in joy. Her brother's best friend had come to save her.

"Gary," she said on an exhale, launching herself into his arms.

He remained silent, as he was known to do. She closed her eyes, squeezing back the tears of relief at having his famous bear hug wrapping her tightly in his embrace. If there was one person she trusted, besides her brother, it was Gary.

He'd been the solid body she'd clung to during her teenage years when life seemed too cruel to handle alone. Later, he'd become her protector when drunk guys hit on her at the clubs. He always lent her an ear when she needed to talk, and he listened without judgment.

"Sorry to hear about the job, Ang." He inhaled deeply, expanding his chest; she could barely get her arms around him.

She leaned back so she could gaze up at his face. "They picked that asshole Rodden over me to go to Germany to open the new shop. Can you believe that? The guy's rough with his hands and has the bedside manners of a stuck-up prick. The least they could've done is keep the spa open here in Seattle, instead of closing. My clientele alone would've been enough to make it profitable."

He chuckled. "Asshole? Prick?"

"Drew's rubbing off on me. Shop talk—go figure." She shuddered. "What are you doing here?"

She reluctantly stepped away from him and forced her shoulders back. Glad to have someone she knew to talk with, she wasn't going to scare him off by bitching. He gave her hand one more squeeze before letting go.

"I thought I'd stay a couple days, see your brother, and pester you." He motioned for her to walk with him.

"I'm not even going to rise to the bait. I'm seriously lacking in any intelligent conversations. The only things people here talk about are hay prices and how many days until winter." She leaned closer and touched him again to make sure she wasn't hallucinating. "Besides, I get you all to myself. Drew's out on business and won't be home until tomorrow."

"Damn. I'd hoped he'd be around." He pointed to the restored Camaro in the driveway of Drew's house behind the garage. "I wanted to see if he could check the muffler. It's riding rough, and sounds like it's made for the racetrack."

"Ugh. Don't talk cars. That's all I hear about twenty-four/seven. Between the gas station and Drew, I've heard enough to last a lifetime." She walked up the driveway, and noticed his bags lying by the front door. "I am so glad you're here."

"Maybe I should hit the motel." He stopped and put his hand on his car. "I'll come by tomorrow and spend some time with you both."

"Are you crazy?" She grabbed his hand. "I just said this place is boring me to tears. Stay at the house and fill me in on what's happening in the Emerald City. Then I want to pick your brain about places I can send my résumé and—" she swallowed "—afterward, I want to hear what is going on with you."

"Same old thing. Training, meetings, and football." He winked. "What you should do is stay with your friend Jules while you search for a job, so you're in the city and closer to a bigger job market. Nowadays, you almost have to be the first one to apply to get the job and that requires being on location."

"I can't. I already asked her last month if she could do me a favor and let me mooch off her until I find employment. She can't do it. She needs a paying roommate in order to afford the rent." She pouted. "Besides, she's already found a roommate since I left…one with a job."

"Too bad."

She leaned into his arm. "I'm stuck here, unless you're looking to help a family friend out and don't mind having a roommate who can't afford to pay you for a few weeks."

"Absolutely not."

"But, Gary…" She gazed up at him and gave him the saddest, most pathetic look she could muster. "You wouldn't even see or hear me. I'll pay you the back rent once I land a job."

"No."

"I'll clean your house."

"Unlike you, I'm not messy." He laughed. "I don't need a maid."

She glared. "Come on, please?"

"No way." He shook his head. "I've got enough going on with my life. Pre-season practice starts in two weeks."

"Some friend you are. I'd let you stay here if you wanted." She snorted. "What a joke. This place would drive you insane in a week's time."

"Women. Never satisfied." He grunted and thumped the roof of the car as they walked by. "Let's go in the house. I'm beat, and the trip was killer."

Tears came to her eyes. This time she didn't have to fake them. Frustration boiled inside her. She was getting desperate enough to hide in his trunk on the way back to Seattle. Once they arrived, he'd have no choice but to let her stay in his mansion of a condominium.

"Give it up, Ang. The answer's no."

She followed him toward the house. "You don't know what I'm thinking."

"I do." He tugged a strand of her hair and looped it behind her ear. "I've known you too long."

"Whatever." She squeezed past him into the room.

Inside the one-story rambling ranch house, the living room sat in disarray. She'd littered the area with all her belongings, and hadn't found the energy to clean since Drew left a week ago.

There was a pillow and blanket thrown haphazardly on the couch, where she'd curled up to watch a movie in the middle of the night when she couldn't sleep. She hurried over and grabbed her things. Then she threw the contents on a pile of boxes near the fireplace.

"Sorry for the disaster zone." She kept her back turned to Gary, and pushed the box of books out of the middle of the living room. "I'll just move—" she grunted "—everything out to the garage."

"Leave it. I'll help you move everything later. Although, it seems messed up that Drew didn't at least get you situated in a bedroom. Are you sure you haven't killed him, or run him off his own property?" He gripped her shoulders, turned her around, and stared into her eyes. "Tell me you didn't drive him over the edge in three months?"

"No, but I'm taking that as a challenge." She grinned wickedly. "I bet that I can crack you in twelve hours."

"You're probably right." His smile disappeared, and he ran his hand over the top of a box. "So, why is all your stuff in the living room?"

"We moved everything out here when Dad dropped Willie and Desiree off here last week for a couple of days, and they took over my bedroom," she said. "I think my lil bro and sis brought every toy they owned with them."

"You love the chaos." He pointed to the couch. "Sit. Relax."

She plopped down on the couch. "I need excitement in my life that comes from people over the age of twenty-one."

"Well, don't wish too hard. A busy life gets old too." He scratched his chest. "Is there beer in the fridge?"

She shrugged. "I don't know. I haven't looked."

"When did you say Drew left?" He walked across the great room, opened the fridge, and pulled out two bottles of beer.

"Uh, five…six days ago." She rubbed her forehead. "Each miserable day is the same. I might've lost track."

"And you don't know what's in the fridge? What have you been eating?" He twisted the cap off both drinks and passed her one. "Here."

"Thanks." She held the drink in her lap, not lifting it to her mouth. "I eat…stuff."

"Dammit." He stalked back into the kitchen. "Get in here and sit your butt down at the counter."

She stood, walked over to the bar stool, and sat. "Why are you mad?"

"You need to eat wholesome food." He searched the cabinets, and took out a half loaf of bread and a jar of peanut butter. "You had no business jogging if you're not taking care of yourself. You'll make yourself sick—or pass out.

"I've eaten," she mumbled, raising the beer to her mouth.

"What?" He stared at her an extra beat. "Your usual junk?"

"If you have to know, I've eaten two bags of Doritos. Family size." She pointed to the empty bags on the counter. "Nacho flavored, which means there's cheese in it, so I'm getting my calcium."

"That's it?" He shook his head as he plunged a knife into the peanut butter.

"No. I also ate a few of those Little Debbie cupcakes, and the vending machines at The Gas Station have already-made sandwiches. The ham and cheese ones are pretty good." She lifted her chin. "You didn't come back here to complain about my diet, have you?"

"Eat this." He put the sandwich in front of her.

She wrinkled her nose. "I'm not hungry."

"Tough. You need some protein to restore your energy. You're practically dragging your feet." He opened the freezer and dropped a package of frozen meat on the counter. "When you're done with that you'll have a proper dinner."

Gary peeled the butcher paper away, and put a solid chunk of steaks on a plate in the microwave. Angie blinked. "I can't eat all that."

"Honey, only one of those is yours." He turned back around and winked. "It was a long trip, and I'm starving."

She smiled and a short laugh escaped. It was the first real happy sound that had come from her in over a week and surprisingly, it felt good; comforting.

"It's so nice to have you here." She leaned her elbows on the counter. "How long can you stay?"

"Well, here's the thing." He pulled a sack of potatoes out from under the sink. "I've got two days until I'm due for a press conference, so I'm spending the time here. I wish I would've called first, because I was really hoping to catch up with Drew. Between his work and my football, we struggle to get together on a regular basis."

She chewed the last bite of her sandwich, swallowed, and brushed the crumbs from her lips. "At least you'd get to see me almost weekly at the clubs…you know, if I was in Seattle."

"Stop trying to talk me into letting you stay with me." He looked away from her. "It wouldn't be a good idea."

He was hiding something from her. She knew him too well, and he'd been off his game since he'd arrived. More mellow and quiet. His usual easygoing attitude and teasing seemed forced, and every time he looked at her, he quickly looked away. She studied him closely. She'd bet anything he hadn't come to see Drew about fixing his car's muffler. It was something else that had brought him here.

"Oh, no." She cradled her forehead in her hand. "Did you get in trouble?"

He glanced at her. "No. Why would you ask that?"

"I just think something huge brought you to Deadhorse, and your excuse of bringing your car for Drew to look at is lame. It'd take more than that to make me come here." She shrugged. "Something's up, and you can tell me. I won't tell a soul."

"You'll have to wait. I want to tell you when Drew's here." He opened the microwave and removed the defrosted meat. "Besides, I don't want to talk about what brought me here yet when I haven't heard about all the exciting things you've been doing."

"Cruel, Satchel, cruel. My life would kill a man like you." She pushed the broiler pan across the counter. Then she realized whatever he had to share with them must be bothering him more than he was saying, because he'd made the long trip from Seattle to Eastern Oregon.

Three months of bad news was more than a single person should have to put up with, and she'd reached her quota. She watched, fascinated, as Gary stripped the potatoes of their peels. Whatever had happened, she could help. She only had to convince him to let her tag along when he went back home.

In the mood for more Crimson Romance?
Check out *The Look-Alike Bride* by Kathryn Brocato at
CrimsonRomance.com.

Printed in Great Britain
by Amazon.co.uk, Ltd.,
Marston Gate.